LOVING THE DON

A SINGLE DADDY NANNY ROMANCE

MICHELLE LOVE

CONTENTS

Blurbs   v

Chapter 1   1
Chapter 2   10
Chapter 3   15
Chapter 4   23
Chapter 5   38
Chapter 6   46
Chapter 7   60
Chapter 8   73
Chapter 9   83
Chapter 10   92
Chapter 11   99
Chapter 12   104
Chapter 13   109
Chapter 14   115
Chapter 15   125
Chapter 16   129
Chapter 17   137
Chapter 18   149
Chapter 19   157
Chapter 20   162

About the Author   167

Made in "The United States" by:

Michelle Love

© Copyright 2020

ISBN: 978-1-64808-590-1

ALL RIGHTS RESERVED. No part of this publication may be reproduced or transmitted in any form whatsoever, electronic, or mechanical, including photocopying, recording, or by any informational storage or retrieval system without express written, dated and signed permission from the author

 Created with Vellum

BLURBS

I've got a thing for sweet girls that are good with my kid ... and Daniela is just my type.

... Too bad I can't love her.
Two years ago, I lost my wife. My love, my little girl's mother. My heart died that day.
Daniela's wonderful: the sweetness of her body, the kindness of her soul. I want to take her to paradise every night. But she's not my wife.
She's just my lover and my friend. And my child's caregiver.
I wish I could love her. She deserves love. She deserves everything.
But all I can give her is great sex and a fat paycheck.

Now an old enemy has declared war. Killed my father. Made me Don—with a deadly fight brewing.
And Daniela is pregnant with my child.
I have no choice but to marry her. But what kind of monster marries a woman knowing he can never give her love?

Daniela deserves more than I can give her. It's too soon after losing my wife.
But when my enemy puts her life in danger, I'll give whatever it takes to save her.

∽

1

Daniela

When I was a small girl, my grandmother raised me on stories of how the Rossinis saved our family from the fascists. I didn't really understand what fascism was, or why these people killed half my family before the rest managed to flee to America. At the time, I thought they were like the monstrous army from *Lord of the Rings*—all hair and tusks and tiny glaring eyes. I didn't know that they were men.

Nonna told me that they didn't like our heritage and that they didn't like our politics or the fact that my great-grandmother had married a Frenchman. She also said that the fascists wanted our money and our land. But the law kept us from leaving. The only people we could rely on to save us were those who lived outside the law.

La Famiglia. The men, we all know about, but nobody talks about. The Rossinis were the only heroes our family could find. And now—decades later and under much different circumstances—they're the only people that I can go to.

As a kid, I used to wonder what it was like for my grandparents and their families to cross the vast black sea on freighters bound for New York Harbor. They had to leave almost everything behind and sold their land to the only men in Sicily with the strength to face the fascists. My family became Americans by the skin of our teeth, begging for asylum beside a million others, most of whom were turned away.

We were among the lucky ones. I wonder, now, if the Rossinis didn't grease those wheels as well. But whatever they did, it saved my family.

"These new gangsters, with their fancy cars and their big guns, they don't know what the old families from Sicily and Barri were really like. How much they did for people. Daniela, those are tough, dangerous men—but sometimes you need tough, dangerous men. We will always owe the Rossini crime family our lives." Nonna's words ring in my ears as I take the off-ramp and head for the Upper East Side.

I park my battered Volkswagen two blocks away

from the gates of the Rossini's massive limestone townhouse and walk the rest of the way, shading my face with my old umbrella to keep from sweating off my makeup. The July sun is merciless today, and I have to look my best. I make sure to hide the ratty umbrella in the bushes before walking up to the intercom to press the button.

"If you ever need work, Daniela, if you're ever desperate, you can go to them. They'll give you an ordinary job with good pay. All you have to do is never talk about what you see or hear there." Nonna told me that a few years after Mom and Dad's funeral, when she was just starting to get sick.

I never thought I would actually take her advice. But here I am, a girl who has never had so much as a parking ticket, about to beg for a job from the most powerful crime family in New York City.

I just hope that, three generations later, they haven't degenerated into a bunch of scumbags like all the other mobsters Nonna used to complain about.

I take a moment to pull myself together and check myself in my compact mirror as I wait for a response. The old compact, with its rose gold case and silver mirror, was left to me in Nonna's will. She's gone now, just like everyone else, or I would be going to my own family instead. What the fascists couldn't take from my family, time, illness, and bad luck have.

I look all right, I think, as I check the mascara around my wide blue eyes. My small mouth is painted a demure shade of rose; with my dark hair and pale skin, I can't wear dark lipstick or I instantly look Goth.

There is a click, and the two cameras at the gate angle in at me like the eyes of a chameleon. "May I help you?" a calm female voice asks.

"Um, I have an appointment with Mr. Rossini today, about the job opening? I'm Daniela—"

"Right," her voice cuts in. "Look at the camera for a moment?"

I raise my face to it, holding still. I don't know if she's checking me against the ID image I emailed them or doing something more esoteric, like using facial recognition. I know she won't find anything suspicious in my background anyway, no matter how deep she digs. But that doesn't keep my stomach from jumping around.

"All right, Miss Orsino, welcome to the Rossini mansion. Please proceed down the path to the main entrance. My office is the first door down the left-hand hallway." There is a buzz and a click, and the gate swings open.

I focus on calming myself as I walk down the crushed shell driveway, determined to land this job. I have no choice. If I end up on welfare, I'll be sleeping in my car.

"Be strong, Daniela," I murmur, walking with care so I don't scuff my one good pair of work shoes. "You can do this."

The townhouse, built from slabs of limestone, looms above the narrow, black-fenced garden surrounding it. It's a Gilded Age wonder, its arched windows gleaming in the sun. I step up onto the gorgeously tiled porch and look in through the glass-paned doors at the foyer beyond. It's as grand as a theater lobby: tile, white walls, a grand staircase with red carpeting, and a hallway branching from either side.

No one is waiting for me on the other side of the door, and that makes my stomach flip again with nervousness. *No, wait, she said to come in and come to her office. I'll just go in.*

Saying a soft prayer under my breath, I push the door open and walk inside. The air inside is fresh and cool and drier than it is outside. I sigh with relief and turn hurriedly toward the hallway on my left.

"Well, hello there." A deep purr of a male voice caresses my ears. I look up the vast sweep of the main staircase and see a tall figure standing there. And suddenly, I can't draw a full breath.

I'm staring up into the greenest eyes I have ever seen. Narrow and amused, they're set in a lean, tanned face with a Roman nose and sensual mouth. There are threads of gold in those eyes, and threads of bronze in the deep brown curls spilling to his shoulders. He's wearing a black Italian suit, cut slim around his lean, dancer's body, with a blazing-white shirt and no tie.

His lips curve into a lazy smile as he sees my eyes widen. "Lovely. I didn't know we were expecting guests."

I swallow, searching desperately for something to say, knowing exactly who he is and wanting desperately to impress him. I want to tell him anything but the truth: that I'm here to work for his family. But as I meet his piercing gaze, I know at once that I can't lie to him. He'll know.

"Um, Mr. Rossini? I called earlier," I confess finally, blushing deeply. "About the nanny job. Your assistant Gina took my call."

"Oh," he says in mild surprise, eyebrows rising as his feral-looking eyes sweep over me. I've worn my best dress, which I usually save for weddings or other special occasions. The soft plum A-line with its empire waist flatters my pale skin and generous curves without being too revealing. Under his eyes, though, I wish I had the money for something better ... and sexier.

"Ah, there you are." Gina's voice rings down the hall and I jump slightly before looking her way. Her voice is as cool, deep, and authoritative as a six-foot cop's ... but she's about four and a half feet tall, chubby, and looks like she could be someone's grandmother. "Sir, this is Daniela Orsino."

"Yes, we were just ... getting acquainted." His eyelids lower lazily as he gives me an amused smile. He walks down the stairs slowly, never breaking our locked gaze, and the closer he gets, the harder my heart pounds.

This is not a reaction I'm familiar with. I'm a virgin; I've always been pretty devout, and I've never dated much. Plus, I'm pretty shy around men, which I'm forcibly reminded of as Mr. Rossini's lazy smile sends a blush across my cheeks. My sexual experience level has pretty much been stuck at novice since I hit puberty.

But right now, I'm falling into those emerald and gold eyes—and I know at once that I'm in trouble. I have no defense against this man ... and if things work out, he's about to be my boss. *And I shouldn't be thinking about fucking my boss!*

"Good. I have her file here." The small woman steps briskly between us, breaking the spell. She hands him a thin manila folder, and he glances at her distractedly and nods. She steps to his side and faces me, offering a supportive smile—and then eyeing her boss like she's worried he's about to misbehave.

He opens the folder, licking his fingertips to turn

the pages and winking at me once. I suck air quietly, dizzy and not sure how to feel. He's incredibly hot. He's hitting on me.

This is not something that happens in my life. It's as powerful as it is unexpected, and I can barely keep my composure under its influence. That saucy smile of his, as his gaze slides over my body, makes me shiver with desire for him.

But we're at a job interview. One that could make or break me.

Of all the times, why does this have to be happening now? With him?

"Orsino. You're on the family list from the old country." He's either reading very fast or barely skimming what's there. "You have any experience with small children?"

"Two nanny jobs, multiple babysitting jobs, and helping to raise my cousins. My references are on the last page." I don't know how I keep what I'm saying from sounding forced. It's hard to talk when someone's stealing your breath.

His posture is relaxed as he pages through the thin examples of my talents and qualifications. I know I can do this—I've always been good with kids—but if someone with a better-looking résumé has already applied, I may end up in the kitchens or something instead.

Fine, so be it. Better peeling potatoes than dumpster diving for my food.

He looks from the folder to me and back again, and he lifts an eyebrow slightly. "Any problems with moving in and starting by tomorrow?"

My heart leaps into my throat and suddenly I can't talk. I just shake my head.

"Good." He licks his lips, and his eyes sweep over me again. "I'll take you, then."

I smile mutely, a tingle running through my body as I wonder how many meanings that statement has.

2

Armand

The decision to seduce my daughter's new nanny is made the moment I look into those big blue eyes of hers and see them dilate with desire. She's got great qualifications, she's from a family that owes us, and her background check came up ridiculously clean. She'll be great for my Laura. No, I'm not hiring her just because I want to fuck her.

But I'm definitely going to.

Sweet, virginal, blushing Daniela, soft-voiced and gentle. I'm watching her introduce herself to my baby now as we stand upstairs in the bright playroom. I'm smiling gently, for my daughter's sake, keeping a close eye on how they interact.

I hired her in minutes, and I was prepared to fire her just as fast if Laura didn't respond well to her.

When Laura lit up when Daniela entered the room, instead of shrinking, I had my first real hope in months. Now I'm watching how gentle and sensitive Daniela is with her, and how encouraging, and I know I made the right choice.

And the whole time I watch Daniela, I'm wondering what her mouth will taste like. Her reaction to me yesterday was so strong that I doubt it would take much to coax her into bed. I wonder if she's ever had a man please her properly before.

But for now, she's working a welcome bit of magic with my shy little Laura. I drag my mind out of my boxer briefs and start calculating a nice hiring bonus.

Laura has never fully recovered from her mother's death. And I can't blame her—I haven't either. It happened in front of us, after all.

Bella went up in the same goddamn fireball that took out Jimmy and his wife, the one I had to shield Laura from with my body as we flew back into the rosebushes. We both climbed out of the debris, screaming for her ... but she was gone.

Everything's been a bit broken since then. I meted out my own form of justice by killing the guy who did it, but I couldn't comfort Laura by telling her that. It wouldn't have comforted her anyway.

I could only tell her that Mama and her aunt and uncle died too damn fast to have possibly felt anything.

Which is probably true. I have to remind myself of that whenever I wake up in the night, reaching for Bella, and feel only an empty space.

Laura's a good kid—smart, especially for a five-year-old. But she's shy, and sadder than any child should be. She's also got it in her head that people don't like her. I'm glad as hell that she's responding well to Daniela's warmth.

I don't know the first goddamn thing about parenting, and I haven't had much help. Mother is busy with six other kids, and Father is busy running this town. I was raised to be the next Don, not a single dad.

I love Laura, though. I do my best with the time I have, but she needs a lot more—and she also needs a good woman to show her how to be one. Mother is already raising Jimmy's kids, now that he's gone, so that means a nanny.

"Can I show you what I drew?" Laura asks Daniela timidly, holding the drawing pad close against her little chest.

Daniela gives her a warm smile and settles into a small chair so she's at eye level with Laura. "Sure, sweetie, let's have a look."

I have to look away—and turn my hips away slightly, too, because I'm hung too big to hide the bulge growing in my pants. The sensible part of my mind is saying, *not again, Armand, you know better,* but it's too goddamned late. Seeing her coax a smile out of Laura within minutes gives me a blue-steel boner almost instantly.

Gina and my mother always scold me about my habit of bedding Laura's nannies. I know it's caused problems in the past. We have been through five of them in the last two years, not counting Maggie, who was sixty and ended up retiring from ill health after ten months. But the rest?

Young women, kind women, who loved children, some a bit plain, some quite pretty, but all of them good with my baby daughter, whose heart has been so hurt. Maybe it's some primal male thing to be attracted to women who will treat my children right. But I couldn't resist a single one of them.

All of them wanted me, and all of them got me. I have a high libido. They were very, very satisfied.

But all of them quickly came to want more out of me than what I could give them—good sex, friendliness, and a paycheck. Even knowing about Bella, hearing my warnings and seeing me always dressed in black, they always ended up wanting my heart, not just my cock. And that can't happen. I buried my heart with the ashes of my wife.

So they left. And Gina and Mother blame me. Which I guess is fair.

Maybe Daniela will leave too—maybe even for the

same reason. I hope not, though. Twenty minutes in, and Laura already likes her.

Problem is that makes her irresistible to me. I adjust myself subtly as I face the window and take a shuddering breath. I should be thinking of something mundane: the new clothes I need to buy for Laura, her desire for a pet, Mother's birthday.

Instead, I'm thinking of sinking my cock into Daniela's soft, warm body, and satisfying the plea I see in those gentle eyes. And that thought, that idea, keeps slipping back into my head no matter how hard I push it away. I have to admit ... I haven't wanted a woman this much since I lost Bella.

So, I'm going to seduce her. Completely, joyously, until we're both tired of each other. And I'm going to find a way to do it without my baby girl losing someone else.

Maybe pleasing Daniela enough is the key. That, and scrupulous honesty. If she doesn't get too dazzled, and I'm careful with her, things could really go well this time.

As I look back over my shoulder at her, I know I need to take the risk. I can already tell that Daniela will be worth it.

3

Daniela

"And this is your room," Armand Rossini, my new boss and crush, says a bit grandly as he unlocks the tall, paneled wood door.

The small suite on the other side doesn't look like servants' quarters, though it is tucked in next to Laura's bedroom. The single long room, with a door to a bathroom on the far end, consists of a sitting room and bedroom with a tiny kitchenette near the front door. The high ceiling and gleaming windows give it an airy, romantic look. The brass bed, with its amber and white bedding, stands as the centerpiece to the whole space.

I pause a few steps past the doorway and look around, my one shabby bag of good clothes clutched in my hands. Armand hasn't commented on the sight of the bag, my umbrella, or my aging car, which he had me drive around through the service entrance and into their garage. In the middle of all this finery, my plain outfit and shabby bag stand out embarrassingly.

This is too rich for me, I think nervously, but I don't let on to him what I'm feeling.

"Will it do?" comes the voice at my ear. He doesn't touch me, but he's standing close enough that he easily could, and the very possibility makes me shiver.

I think about my tiny closet of a room in Nonna's house, now taken by the bank. I think about my parents' apartment before their deaths, and how I had no room—only a roll-away cot under their bed. And for a moment, before I catch myself, I'm ashamed.

"It's lovely," I say simply, moving further into the room. For a moment, I don't know if he's going to come in with me, but then I hear his footstep enter the room and the door shutting. And suddenly I'm alone, behind closed doors, with this magnificent man, wrestling with my feelings.

Okay. He's my boss. But he's straight-up flirting with me.

On the clock, I'm his subordinate. But off the clock, with Laura now down for her afternoon nap and the reality of my new life setting in, he's an incredibly attractive man with an interest in me. And I have to figure out what to do about that.

"So, I didn't ask you," Armand says as he walks up behind me. "How did you end up making that call to Gina, anyway? You're a bit squeaky clean to be working for a family like mine."

The irony in his voice doesn't escape me. I turn an awkward smile on him, hugging the bag to my chest. "I was staying with my grandmother while I went to college. She was the only relative I had left. Once she was gone, I didn't have many options."

"I see," he murmurs thoughtfully, and I fight the urge to look away again. He isn't commenting on my poverty, but rather on my innocence. And that's nothing to be ashamed of; I'm twenty, not forty.

"When my great-grandfather decided to take as many families as he could out of Italy with us, it became ... something of a family legend. But most of the families just went their own way afterward. I think the family business scares them off.

"I admit that when we get someone from those families coming to us, it's always a bit of a surprise." That thoughtful tone doesn't waver as I settle into a gold-upholstered chair and he stretches lazily across the matching loveseat across from me. "Aren't you scared of us?"

His question, and the way he lounges with hooded eyes, like a sleepy cat, is so mild and flirtatious that I'm unsure of how to respond. Finally, I reply, "Your family saved mine. That might have been generations ago, but we remember. I've got no problem working for you as long as it doesn't involve hurting anyone."

He sits back, chuckling. "That will never happen. You're here for my daughter, and that is all. Of course, when you go out with her, you will need to take one of my men with you if I'm not available. You might want to consider taking one when you are out by yourself as well. Things are a bit ... hot ... on the streets right now."

I blink, setting down my bag, slightly shocked. "I never considered that. Are the people who work for you usually in danger just for ... being the help?"

"Not usually. But you need to understand. We have honor. Our rivals ... don't." He straightens and his tone becomes more serious. "They try to use that to their advantage, as if honor is a weakness.

"So that means sometimes a maid, or a nanny, or, one time, our goddamn pizza delivery guy, gets kidnapped, or threatened, or what have you. They think that we can be intimidated by threatening our employees' safety."

I let out my breath in a rush, only now aware that I was holding it. "What happens then?"

"My father has our people rescued, and then we come down hard on the kidnappers. Our sense of mercy is only extended toward the innocent, you see."

His gleaming eyes search my face as he speaks, and I feel another tingle run through me.

"I guess you should introduce me to some of your guys, then. It will be weird running errands with a bodyguard, but ... I don't really fancy being kidnapped." I smile awkwardly, and he lets out a soft laugh, the darkness receding from his expression.

"You're a genuine treasure," he says, and I blush down to my toes. "This should work well. You have a general understanding of how things should work, I don't have to worry about your ethics or your brains, and Laura likes you already."

"Well, I hope so. I like her." I blink and hesitate, wondering how much I can ask about that sweet but timid little girl without being nosy. "She does seem a touch ... quiet. Does she have any conditions or issues that I should know about?"

His smile fades, and he nods, glancing out the window as a cardinal lands on a branch outside. "She saw her mother die. We both did. It's been a few years, but you don't really get over something like that. Certainly not so quickly."

I swallow, my eyes wide with horror and concern. Not just for the little girl whose care is now partly in my hands, but for the man in front of me, whose fierce eyes glance so briefly away in grief. "What ... should I do to make things easier on her?"

"Don't leave," he replies almost at once. "She's had too many people leave on her."

I nod mutely, not sure what to say. I have no plans to leave. In fact, I have no idea where I would even go. But now I have a reason to stay, besides my own desperation.

... And my growing crush on the man sitting across from me, of course.

"I'll introduce you around to everyone later, and give you a few people you can call on for a ride and escort. Right now I'm afraid most of the staff is unavailable. We're preparing for a party this evening. I'll need you to keep Laura occupied until her bedtime, and stay nearby afterward." The instructions come out smoothly, and I nod.

"I should get settled tonight anyway." The fact that this is really happening is still sinking in. I'm not going to be homeless. I'll still have to skip school for the semester, but if I save up for a year, I can start paying my own tuition. "I do have one question ..."

I look up to see him leaning toward me, elbows on knees, eyes fixed on me with the intensity of a curious cat. "Go on."

"Would it be possible for me to have a place to paint? I'm sure you don't want oil paints in the bedrooms." I give him an awkward smile.

My painting gear is still in my locker back at school

—if they haven't thrown it out. I only withdrew from classes three days ago, though. I'm hoping I have time to retrieve it.

"You teach my little girl some basics of painting, and I'll make sure you have a whole studio." He glanced at the bag. "Didn't see you come in with any painting gear, though."

"It's on campus," I admit. I still can't hide anything from him. "Everything else is in here."

His jaw drops, his suave exterior crumbling a touch from astonishment. "This is it? Did you go through a house fire?"

I close my eyes, the sudden ache that shoots through me so intense that I press my hand over my heart. Three nights ago, the bank sent cops. Nobody got in touch with me; nobody warned me it was coming.

"Pretty much," I mumble.

Five minutes. The cops gave me five minutes to grab everything that I could, or they would arrest me for trespassing. What the hell was I supposed to grab? Clothes, my battered laptop, Nonna's locket, a few photos? The folder with my birth certificate?

"What happened?"

I look up at him, my attraction and loneliness warring with my good sense. I want so much to confide in him, but I don't want to look weak in front of him. Finally, I just give him the facts.

"My grandmother died, and the bank took our house. I got kicked out with no warning by the cops three days ago." I look down and realize my hands are clenched tightly together, and loosen my grip.

"Oh." His eyes flick down to the bag again. "My condolences. I'll talk to you tomorrow about purchasing some new things."

Another surprise. "That's not necessary—" I start, but he simply holds up a hand as he rises.

"Nonsense, what you have here isn't enough. It'll be on my dime, don't worry." He winks as he pushes himself to his feet. "For now, you'll dine with Laura tonight in the kitchen. Her bedtime is eight. Your time is your own after that, as long as you don't stray from your rooms."

He fishes out a card and hands it to me. "The current WiFi password. It's changed twice a week. I'll make sure you get the updates."

Our fingers brush as I take the card, and I feel the contact down to my toes. Then he's gone again, stepping out and closing the door behind him.

4

Armand

I want to spend the rest of the afternoon getting to know lovely little Daniela, but duty calls. Or rather, my mother does.

I make my way up to the palatial top floor, where my mother rules and rarely descends outside of parties and mealtimes. My shoes make no sound on the thick red carpet as I walk up to the door of her library.

"Mother? You summoned me?" I already know what it's about, but it's probably best to play innocent anyway.

My mother puts her copy of *Faust* down and slips a gilt bookmark between its pages. "I hear that you hired a new nanny for my granddaughter." She looks up at me with her sharp black eyes. "I trust that you did not just hire her for her looks."

"I never do, Mother, and you know that," I say patiently, squashing my irritation. "Daniela is quite competent, and Laura took to her right away. You can check in on them yourself whenever you want."

My mother is a severe-looking but elegant woman, her thick iron-colored hair twisted into elaborate braids that coil at her nape. Her lavender and silver dressing gown always smells faintly of the cigarettes she sneaks on the sly now and again. I frown, knowing what that smell means.

"Something's bothering you." She only ever smokes when she's stressed.

She sighs and removes her gold-rimmed spectacles, eyeing me. "Armand, your father and I have been discussing it, and we want you to take over more of his duties. You know that your father's health isn't what it used to be. You need to prepare yourself to take over for him anyway."

I hesitate, feeling a faint catch in my chest. "The doctor's visit didn't go so well, huh?"

She smiles tightly. "No. Don't ask him about it. He's angry because the doc wants him to give up cigars." She waves a hand. "I already told him he shouldn't be smoking with his diabetes."

I take a deep breath. "What duties, in particular?"

"More of the face-to-face stuff. Accepting payoffs. Checking in with the boys. Delivering some of our communications to our rivals when we need to make an impression. We want you to start playing more of a public role." She's still staring at me.

I stare back. "What aren't you saying, Mother?"

"Well, it's been two years now, and as much as I understand you mourning your wife, you have your future position to consider. If you want our men, allies, and rivals to view you as a respectable leader in La Famiglia, you must be married. You know that."

A shock goes through me. "I can't believe you're bringing this up. Would you want Father to remarry after only two years if you died?"

She nods once, grimly. "Yes, I would. The Don is always a family man, you know that. The rest of our family won't even take you seriously if you're running around screwing nannies instead of being settled down and married."

I rub my temple. "Not this again."

"Yes, this again. I saw that gleam in your eye when you walked in. This new one—Daniela, wasn't it? She's quite pretty, but you need to keep your head on straight. She's here for your daughter, not for you."

I set my teeth together in a forced smile. "I'm aware of that, Mother."

"It's actually good for you to be attracted to women who are good with your daughter. But what's going to come of all this sex without commitment? Bastards,

Armand. You know that." She throws up her hands in disgust.

"That actually hasn't happened," I protest, but she shakes her head.

"It's only a matter of time. You're just like your father. You think I ended up with eight kids because we planned it that way?"

I open my mouth to mention that, unlike my father, I don't let the pope scare me off of using condoms ... but shut it again. *Bad idea.*

I can face down a dozen armed enemies. I can stay cool as an autumn night when questioned by the cops. But Italian mothers are a different sort of ferocious. They have you by the heart and the conscience, and they damn well know it.

"Ma, you have nothing to worry about," I reassure her. "There aren't going to be any bastards."

"There had better not be, or you're marrying the girl. You need a wife anyway."

I sigh and nod. "I understand." I don't, though. My sex life is my private business, family obligations or not. But I do understand that the only way out of this conversation is to sound like I'm conceding.

"You go upstairs to see the Queen Mother?" Tony teases me as I walk down into the foyer with an irritated expression ten minutes later.

I roll my eyes at him. "Yep."

He laughs, his soft brown eyes dancing. Tony is huge and a touch round—a bear of a man, and the only guy who works for me who keeps a full beard. "Say no more. Gina has a briefing for you. Says I should come along."

"Thanks. C'mon then." *Shit.* I hoped to have the afternoon to flirt with Daniela, and maybe take her out to buy some clothes and things. I still can't believe the fucking bank took her house right after her grandma died. Those are the real crooks.

Looks like duty calls, anyway. I turn down the hall and tap on Gina's office door before entering. She looks up mildly, then stands, her smile all business. Something is up.

"I have already made certain your father knows of this matter, but it's important that you do as well. The Frazettis just killed Fortunato and made his men swear loyalty to Carlo." She slides a folder across to me.

Gina is old school. Her computer is powerful and her computer files immaculate, but we always get a printout handed to us in a manila folder during these meetings. Her way is actually more secure, so I've never complained.

I open the folder and look down at the printout. "This is a copy of the police report." I skim through it. "This is the fourth small-timer he's taken out in two weeks."

"Yes," she said solemnly. "Clearly, Carlo Frazetti is consolidating power wherever he can grab it. And there is only one reason for him to be doing so this aggressively."

"They plan to move on us too," I finish the thought for her. "But they're coming to the party and the meeting tonight. They've been pretending like they want to strengthen ties."

"I know. But there's an eighty-odd percent chance that they've been deceiving us." She looks at me earnestly. "Your father is too busy with receiving his lieutenants to handle the matter of tonight's security." She looks over at Tony. "That is why I asked the two of you to come confer on the matter."

I nod grimly, folding my arms. "Of course. I want every available man on duty. I want half of them on obvious patrol, in uniforms. The rest I want split between staff and party guests. If the Frazettis try anything, no matter how small, they will regret it."

I have no doubt that Father will back my play. It might cost our boys a little sleep, but failing to keep our home and family secure will cost us all a lot more.

I page through the rest of the folder and then look up at Tony. "I know better than to try to talk Father into wearing a vest, but I'll have armored clothing on, and I think our staff and men should have theirs too.

Concealed carry on everyone. Let's not let the bastards know what we're packing."

"What about the new girl?" Tony muses, and I stiffen slightly.

"Background check came up clean. No ties to any family but ours, especially now that her own family's gone." Gina's expression is calm until she catches something in my expression that makes her pause in surprise.

I force a smile. "She's also good with Laura. Tony, seriously, the most unusual thing about her is that she's an art geek. Even if you can't trust my instincts, Gina has this covered."

Tony looks at me for a moment, then nods. "Just saying. Putting a mole on our staff sounds exactly their style."

"True enough. But I'll be watching Daniela closely in any case. She's looking after my daughter, after all." I say this calmly enough—and they both wince. "What?"

"Nothing," Tony says diplomatically.

"The young lady is lovely and kind, at least on the surface. But she is our newest employee. It would be best to be ... careful with her."

Oh for fuck's sake, why is everyone in this household so damn nosy about where my dick goes? I'm in my thirties, not my teens! I smile reassuringly. "Of course."

By the time the sun has set, a line of cars runs all the way up and down our semicircular drive. Luxury cars with smoked windows, some probably armored, all of them showing off the wealth and ego of their owners. Polished men and women, from the darkest dregs of society, mill about on our stairs and fill the second-floor ballroom to capacity.

I stand at the landing above the crowd with Tony beside me, watching the guests file in. My black suit and white tie are of a bespoke ballistic fabric indistinguishable from silk and wool, and I can see a high-end vest adding to Tony's bulk under his suit. "Are the cell-phone jammers in place?"

Tony nods and folds his arms over his barrel chest. "No one's getting a single bar unless they're outside the gates. And I've got the guys linked up on radio."

"Good." I adjust my tie slightly and look down. "I should go mingle before the meeting. It will be expected."

He nods. "Catch up with ya later. I'm gonna check in with the guys."

Parties like this have a very specific purpose. They provide a venue for our loved ones to mingle while men and women from half a dozen or more criminal organizations meet behind closed doors. The proximity of our families helps keep tempers cool and words measured. And more than one alliance, temporary or otherwise, has been cemented because our wives, mothers, or siblings make friends first.

I make my way through the ballroom, watching the crowd. The Frazettis are here in force. I see Carlo sweep past with an entourage of at least ten men. Every eye is upon them—everyone knows by now that Carlo has blood on his hands tonight.

Carlo knows it best. A decade younger than my father, he stalks around on his long legs, sporting gray from head to toe. From his crop of wavy hair; his hard eyes over his hooked nose; his suit; and the pallid, washed-out skin that serves as the only sign of his addiction, he looks like a vampire stalking among my people, and all the men behind him are dressed in black.

In the midst of them, I see a hint of moonlight-colored velvet: Frazetti's spoiled daughter, Alexandra. Beautiful, haughty, and manipulative, she's four years older than me and looks like a Sicilian angel. But her light brown eyes are the sly eyes of a practiced courtesan of old—one with poison hidden in her rings.

My mother once suggested that we marry, to try and heal the rift between our families. Frazetti and my father shared a good laugh over my horrified look as I struggled not to say anything rude. As for Alexandra, she ignored us all and later flirted with Tony in front of his wife.

I pray my mother isn't planning a repeat of her proposal tonight. I'll absolutely have to refuse. She can push me into a lot, but I would rather marry a complete stranger than Alexandra. That woman can kill my boner faster than a shot of Novocain.

As I walk around the room greeting people, I notice that we're nearly at capacity already. My mother sails around playing hostess, the brace on her leg hidden under a long burgundy satin skirt. Nobody but us knows that she had to take the service elevator down. It's important for us to show no weakness of any kind in this room of vipers. Despite our attempts at maintaining alliances, you never know who's just waiting for a chance to take advantage.

Then, suddenly, the hair on the back of my neck prickles, and I know at once who is approaching me. I look up and see Carlo walking over with a broad fake smile on his face and his arms open. "Well, look who graced us with his presence. Rossini the Younger. How are you, Armand?"

I have a million reasons to hate Carlo. Not the least of which is the fact that the man is my bastard cousin and has designs on everything that is my father's—and mine. He knows I know it, and gloats as I greet him politely—but without touching him.

"Good evening, Carlo. I'm well. May I help you with something?" I ask briskly.

"I'm merely inquiring after your health ... and the health of your father." His smile widens while his eyes stare at me like scanners on a machine: no soul in there. Father has told me that he was an enforcer before taking over his side of the family business.

I can believe it. And I wouldn't be surprised if he shot a few of his own kin on his way to the top. "My father's fine, Carlo. You can ask him yourself, after the meeting." I gesture to the tall double doors at the far end of the ballroom.

He looks that way and nods. "Oh, well then, see you at the meeting." And just as quickly as he came, he sweeps off again, giving me his back as if daring me to take a shot at him.

Carlo's the kind of creep who sent me a condolence card for my wife back when he was on the short list of suspects for the bombing. Now he's swanning around my house, in front of my family, with a security team larger than the mayor's.

I don't know when I stopped suspecting him of killing my wife, or at least of being in on it, or when I just started wanting him dead, because I loathe him and think he's a hazard. I watch him glad-handing his way around the room like a politician hunting for votes, and I'm more convinced than ever that he's up to something.

I need a moment with Father before the meeting

starts. Hopefully he's in a listening mood. I start heading for the double doors right away, brushing past Alexandra as she swoops in with two flutes of champagne in hand.

I enter the grand meeting room armored with tired determination, my manner unflappable but my heart heavy. Between my mother's crazy demand that I remarry and the problem with the Frazettis, I have too much to deal with. But I'll bear up and stick by Father's side and play the part of his strong right-hand and heir.

He's at the head of the long, inlaid cherry table as I walk in, with Melissa, his *consigliere*, at his side. She's small, dyes her white hair platinum blonde, and wears a touch too much makeup, but she's as smart as Gina, and twice as deadly in a gunfight. They both give me a smile as I join them, pulling out the chair on my father's right.

"You want to tell me why a third of my men are here in tuxedos and server's uniforms?" my father asks, slyly amused. He's a foot shorter than I am, his heavy muscles gone to fat a bit, and his broad bulldog face full of smiles. I have his green eyes, but thankfully I have my mother's hairline.

"Security needed beefing up. You saw the note?" He nods, and I settle into my seat with a sigh. "They're circling us like hungry jackals."

"Don't let Carlo rattle you," Father soothes, raising a meaty hand. "He's got no chance of taking New York City. He's not even third in line in terms of power."

"But does he know that? He might still try. And if he does, we could take losses." I keep my voice calm and low as the others file in, not wanting to be overheard contradicting the Don in public.

My father nods shrewdly and peers down the table as men and women from four different crime families file into the room. Besides the Frazettis, there are the DeLuccas, our closest allies, a collection of aging giants who control Long Island. Then there are the Capurros, who have negotiated a truce allowing them to keep their piece of the racketeering pie while still kissing Father's ring. And finally, the Corteses, my wife's family, who are the only ones who have helped us in the search for her killer.

Carlo comes in with his men and occupies an entire side of the table. His daughter stuffs herself in next to me and smiles at me vapidly. I give her a polite hello and turn back to my father.

My father calls the meeting to order while I watch distractedly, too aware of the woman staring at me on my other side. The sharing of underworld news that follows contains no information that my sources haven't already brought me. I'm here to keep an eye on the Frazettis ... and ignore whatever it is Alexandra is brewing up next to me.

As Joe DeLucca rambles on about a Puerto Rican gang interfering with their diamond smuggling and how they have taken care of the problem, I watch Carlo's reflection in the bank of windows across from us. He's settled in, an expectant smirk on his face. As the rest of the table discusses what to do about upstart gangs in our territory, he and the rest of the Frazettis are silent.

Like they're waiting for something.

I catch Tony's eye and he nods, speaking briefly into his lapel mic. He's noticed it too. Whatever they try, we're ready.

My thoughts fly immediately to my daughter upstairs—and to Daniela. They will have had dinner by now, and with Gina's help, will have given Laura her bath and her vitamin. Right now is about the time for bedtime stories and sleep.

After that, soft-eyed Daniela will be free ...

I tear my mind away from that and focus back on business, ignoring my suddenly half-awake dick. There will be time for that once the Frazettis have played their hand and failed. I look back up just in time to watch Carlo stand up to take his turn.

"Well, gentlemen, I don't have much to announce

today, aside from a bit of sad news. Fortunato is no longer among us."

"We already know, Carlo," my father breaks in tiredly. "You've been running around picking off small-timers for weeks now, and doing almost nothing to cover your tracks."

Carlo blinks slowly and I have to bite back a laugh. Unfortunately, I'm immediately distracted by a hand on my thigh.

My nascent boner dies immediately as I feel greedy little fingers wander over the muscles of my leg through my pants. Beside me, Alexandra is smiling slyly, glancing at me out of the side of her eye. The hand starts moving north fast, like she's greedy for a fistful of cock.

I give her a disgusted look and remove her hand firmly, tossing it in her lap. She gives the same slow, confused blink as her father gave moments ago, and I wonder if having her clumsily try to seduce me is part of her father's plan.

But no. Something else is up, and I have to be watchful. Who knows what the real plan is?

5

Daniela

I'm restless and wary after putting Laura to bed. She likes me and I like her—I think we're off to a great start. I got her to eat, bathe, and take her vitamin with little help from Gina, who commented on my success with her before leaving. But I still can't shake the feeling that something is wrong.

The feeling only intensifies once I return to my room. In this big, unfamiliar space, however comfortable, I feel weirdly vulnerable. I know that part of it has to be the fact that I'm in a mob family's mansion, but ... there's more to it.

I walk over to my bag and dig into the bottom, pulling out my small box of tampons. The security guy searched my bag but didn't fish inside of it. I don't know what they would think about my hiding my dad's old folding knife among my things, but just having it in my hand makes me feel safer.

But what am I scared of, really? Not Armand. The only thing about him that has me scared is what I'll do if he starts flirting with me again. Probably fall all over myself.

I go to the window and stare out over a rolling lawn lit by the rising moon. It's so beautiful here, and aside from the huge number of cars lining the driveway, it's peaceful. Or seems that way.

The air has gotten stale, and now that the temperature has dropped, the upstairs windows are open to let the night breeze in. It blows strands of my hair around my face as I stare across the grounds of my strange new home. The city shimmers just beyond the fences, but this place feels like an oasis.

Almost.

I wonder how the party is going downstairs. I can't see any part of it spilling out onto the lawn. Now and again I do see an armed guard passing by.

It's probably nothing, I finally decide. I consider turning on the flat-screen television on the wall across from the couch, but I'm not really a TV girl. The prospect of unlimited cable might excite me more if I wanted to watch a movie.

Instead, I log into my laptop and use the password to connect to the Internet and play some streaming radio. I put on The Piano Guys and go back to the window. From four stories up, I can see over most of the trees that line the property.

The view will be pretty to wake up to, I think, and wonder how long it will take me to get used to all of this.

Then I hear something. A thump and a rattling sound, coming from just outside. It sounds like something hit the roof and fell. Frowning, I turn my head—and see something very strange.

There's some kind of rope or cord running from the rooftop down to the lower stories that wasn't there before. It's hanging tautly six inches from one of the open windows to Laura's bedroom. As I watch, it vibrates, then stops.

Then it does it again.

I look down—and to my absolute horror, I see a man starting to use the cord to climb the wall. He's dressed in some kind of dark outfit, turning him into a shadow clinging to the limestone. I know instantly what he's here for—or who, to be more accurate.

Grabbing my knife, I press the security call button on the wall and dash through the connecting door to Laura's room. She's fast asleep, balled up on her bed in a patch of moonlight. As I hurry in as quietly as possible, I can see the rope outside the window, pulling away from the wall and shaking more as the man gets closer.

My eyes narrow. I flick the blade of my knife open. *No, you don't.*

I creep over to the window. I can't wait for security to haul their asses up the stairs. I have to act now.

I hear the man's soft grunts of effort as he climbs. He's getting closer. I have to wait, but not so long that he can grab the windowsill.

I take a deep breath—and shove the window screen open, leaning out and grabbing the cord. "What the fuck?" the guy yelps—and the cord shakes in my grip as he tries to climb faster.

I lash out with the knife, sawing at the rope. I keep it sharp. I cut through in seconds.

"Oh shit—" I hear the man yell in total panic—and then a second later, there's a heavy thud in the bushes below.

He groans. He's alive. "You tried," I mutter as I walk out into the hallway, folding the knife and hiding it in my pocket.

Four huge guys with guns run up just as I close the door. One of them, slightly older-looking, with auburn hair, blinks at me. "What's the problem?"

"Someone tried to break into Laura's room using some damn mountain-climbing gear. He's in the bushes."

He looks back at the other three, who make a dash down the hall for the stairs. "Show me," he says quietly.

We creep inside and I lead him to the window with the open screen—and the sawed-off end of the rope dangling in view. I hear him draw a sharp breath. He leans out the window, looks down—and stifles a laugh.

Lips pressed together, he motions me back out into the hallway. "That's ... definitely a would-be kidnapper. You cut the rope?"

"Of course. What would you have done?" I lean against the wall, slack with relief. I can hear faint shuffles and shouts outside.

"Well, I have a gun. But that would have woken up the kid. We'll take it from here. Mr. Rossini will want to talk to you once we've sorted everything out." He hesitates briefly, then gives me a small smile. "Good job."

I nod silently, starting to shake. *I can't believe I did that.*

I don't want to leave Laura out of my sight, so I enter her room again. I close the screen then sit on the couch in her bedroom, watching her sleep. I'm hoping someone will clue me in on what happened to the intruder, and who he was.

Finally, a little under an hour after I cut that rope, Armand comes in quietly and closes the door. The set of his body is tense. I stand, suddenly worried that I've done something wrong. But he simply brushes past me to check on his daughter and then looks out the window at what's left of the rope.

When he's done, he comes back over and motions for me to follow him into my room. With the door shut, he startles me by gently putting his elegant, long-fingered hands on my shoulders. "Is she all right?" he asks gently.

"She didn't even wake up," I reassure at once.

He looks into my eyes, his gaze piercing. "Are you all right?"

I start to shiver. His hands are so warm on my shoulders, his grip firm but gentle. I try to speak, and all that comes out is a small, soft sound of distress. Only then do I realize just how scared I was until he showed up.

He cups my face gently ... and then a knock at the door distracts us both. "Come in," he snaps, stepping back from me. His whole manner and body language shifts, and suddenly he's all business.

A big, bearded man with receding dark curls lumbers in. "That's it, boss. The Frazettis don't know yet that we caught their guy."

"What's the rundown on what happened?"

"He was their driver. But instead of waiting with the car, he grabbed a goddamn grappling hook, shot it onto the roof with a crossbow, and climbed up the wall with a bag on his back like he thought he was some hero in a spy movie." The big guy spreads his hands. "Your new nanny here called us, then went and cut the rope before he could get in the window."

Armand lets out a small, stunned noise and looks down at me sharply. "Is ... that so?"

I stare up into his eyes for a moment and see them dilate slightly. Something electric passes between us. "Yes," I say softly.

He turns to the other man. "Tony. Bring the driver to the safehouse and treat his wounds. No one is to let on to the Frazettis that we know what happened. Keep cell phones jammed."

He takes a deep breath. "I'm handling this myself. My father is finishing the meeting. We can't tell him in front of Carlo, so keep it quiet with everyone downstairs until the guests leave."

"Won't they notice that their driver is missing?"

Armand shakes his head, frowning. "No. They will have expected him to leave with my daughter. Take his car into the garage and drape it for now." Something dark enters his voice for a moment. "We'll give it back to Frazetti later."

Tony nods and walks out, and Armand locks the door behind him. Then he turns a concerned look on me as the stiffness fades from his stance. "You could have taken a bullet when you leaned out to cut that line."

I take a deep breath, the reality of what happened making me cold all over. But then I lift my chin and look back at him firmly. "I decided that I would rather take a bullet than stand there and let him climb in the window. He probably would have shot me anyway. And then who would have protected your daughter while the guards were still coming up the stairs?"

He takes a shuddering breath and moves toward me again, towering over me. I realize with a shock that he's trembling.

"You …" he murmurs, his hands sliding up my arms and making me shiver. "You're brave, too. How did you get so fucking perfect?"

Then he pulls me into his arms.

6

Daniela

My breath catches as I'm being held so tenderly against Armand's broad chest, his powerful muscles flexing slightly against my body as he cradles me. His heart is pounding even harder than mine, startling me. His grip tightens, but it only makes me feel more secure. He could break me, but his embrace never hurts or makes me feel trapped.

I melt against him, even as he lifts me half off my feet in his enthusiasm. The sudden rush of pleasure and relief is so strong that when his lips brush mine, I offer my own mouth eagerly. A tiny part of me wonders what I think I'm doing—this is my employer, a man I've known for less than two days—but then it gets drowned out completely.

The kiss ebbs and strengthens over and over,

sending tides of tingling warmth through me. I can feel my hands gripping his upper arms as he holds me and I whimper with soft delight against his mouth. It's better than I ever expected a simple kiss to feel. My knees wobble—and then the weight is taken off them entirely.

When the kiss breaks, my feet are off the floor, and he's holding me firmly against him as he buries his face in my neck. His mouth traces over my skin hungrily; I gasp for air, stunned by his sudden explosion of passion. It's like my actions in protecting Laura were the perfect aphrodisiac for this single dad.

I hang onto his shoulders and wrap one leg around his thigh as he covers my neck and collarbones in kisses, my soft gasps and whimpers the only sound in the room. It feels so good ... but the intensity overwhelms me quickly, and I start to tense up.

He backs off gently and lowers me to my feet, but still keeps me in the circle of his arms. "Are you all right?" he asks again, but this time he's panting for air as his eyes search my face.

"I like it," I whisper breathlessly. "But ... it's ... it's so much more than I'm used to." I'm pathetically grateful that he has taken this break. My heartbeat slows, and my anxiety loosens its grip around my throat.

One of his hands comes up and strokes through my hair, soothing me. "Do you want me to stop?"

I close my eyes, taking a shivery breath, trying to think past the erotic daze he's left me in. Even in the midst of his passion, he cares enough to check in with me. It gives me an out ... but it also ensures that I absolutely don't want it.

Belly fluttering with excitement, I open my eyes again and look up into his burning gaze. Coming here for this job was a huge risk, but it paid off big. Now, I'm about to take another one.

"No," I murmur as I slide my palms up his chest. I'm already drunk on the feeling of being close to him. "Don't stop."

I'm a million miles from my old life now—from college and high school and the disappointments and aggressiveness of boys that age. As he shucks his suit jacket, I think back briefly to conversations with my friends about their boyfriends, and the sad, patient frustration with which they described sex.

But those were boys. This is a man.

As he steps out of his dress shoes and gathers me into his arms, the dizzy fear of entering unknown territory makes a last clutch at my stomach before giving up. This is my choice. I've never felt this much desire for any man ... and I want to enjoy it.

He kisses and nuzzles me as he nudges me back toward the bed, his hands sliding up and down my arms and then moving over my back. His fingers are warm through the fabric of my dress, tracing the curves of my body.

He's so gentle, his huge hands caressing me softly, taking his time. His shirt hangs open now, and I slip my hands inside to caress his smooth skin. He shivers under my touch, his muscles tensing under my fingertips. I feel the faint slickness of an old scar on his back, long and barely the width of my finger, but it barely distracts me.

He's kissing my neck, nibbling lightly, running his tongue over my jawline and tracing the lobe of my ear. His fingertips slide over my breasts, and then back behind me, easing the zipper of my dress down.

The backs of my knees press up lightly against the padded edge of the bed just as he slips the dress off my shoulders and tugs it down gently. It falls at my feet, leaving me standing there in my underwear and thigh-high stockings. I wrap my arms around myself in a fit of shyness, but then fight it off, lowering my arms and uncovering myself.

He distracts me from any feelings of self-consciousness as he takes off his shirt and then calmly unbuckles his pants and lets them drop. His body is supple and sleek, all but hairless save for the narrow, dark trail disappearing into the top of his waistband. The clinging indigo silk boxers drape the bulge of his erection as he settles onto the bed behind me.

I look back at him almost timidly—and he scoots forward and lays his mouth against my spine. His tongue and teeth slide over my skin, sending a wave of sensation through me.

I gasp and fall back against him as he runs his hands over my ass and hips, gripping one hipbone while the other brushes very delicately over the front of my panties. That tiny touch makes my pussy tingle. He rubs me lightly there as he chuckles. "You're wet for me already. Good."

He runs his tongue up my spine from tailbone to the bottom of my bra and I gasp, sudden electricity running through me. Only then do I realize that he's tugged my panties off my hips at the same moment. I feel them slide down my thighs and to the floor—and then gasp as he pulls me back against him.

His throbbing bulge brushes against my ass as he runs his hands over my bra-clad breasts. I'm starting to get too turned on to be nervous; the freedom of this pleasure amazes me. I turn to him finally, letting him pull me onto the bed.

He lays me on my back and stares down at me hungrily, slowly pulling his boxers down. His cock springs free against his belly, and my eyes widen slightly. Thick and dark, smooth skin taut and gleaming, it shivers slightly as my gaze falls on it, as if he's aroused further just by my looking at him.

It seems enormous; my hand might not fit all the way around it. Fear pricks at me. *Can I handle this?*

But instead of thrusting into me like I halfway expect, he stops to gently undress me the rest of the way. He unrolls my stockings down my thighs, kissing his way up their insides when he's done, and then nuzzling my pussy teasingly before bending over me again. I can hear his breathing turn harsh.

I brace myself slightly, expecting impatience again … and again, he surprises me pleasantly by reaching for the catch on my bra instead.

I'm wearing a front-fastener in purple satin, my only nice one. He opens it eagerly and pulls the cups aside, eyes lighting up as my full breasts spill out. He cups one almost reverently as I slip out of the bra, then starts covering it with kisses.

I shiver, back arching, my eyes wide open but seeing nothing. No one's touched me in these places before, but here is this hot near-stranger, kissing that sensitive, untouched skin softly, again and again.

He swirls his lips inward slowly, getting closer and closer to my nipple, which goes tight with anticipation. I arch my back, offering myself to him—and am rewarded as he slips his hot mouth over it.

And then he starts to suck, and my mind goes blank for a long moment. I moan and throw my head back, pressing against him eagerly. His arms support me as I arch and tremble helplessly against him. I've never felt this much pleasure in my life ... and I've never felt such a strong desire for more.

"Don't stop ..." I gasp out, unable to draw a full breath anymore. My vision blurs in and out as he teases and kisses my breasts, his hands running over my back and ass. With the last of my self-control, I struggle to keep my sounds of pleasure quiet.

But in minutes, we're both so far gone that I have to muffle myself against the back of my arm.

I'm going wild, my cunt tightening, my nipples so hard and sensitive that they hurt so fucking *good*. He's suckling me hard, greedily, tongue lashing against my nipple as I arch and clutch at his shoulders. The pleasure catches in my lower belly and builds, and my clit aches with need.

"Oh God," I moan. "What are you doing?"

He doesn't answer, but it's clear; his tongue traces down my breastbone and belly as he slowly moves down my body.

Dizzy with arousal, I gasp with disbelief as his tongue circles my navel and then trails lower, past the curve of my belly and down over the trimmed hairs of my pussy. Lower, lower, while his nimble fingers caress me—and his arms and shoulders hold my thighs open firmly.

I feel his warm breath on my clit—and then his

tongue slides over it and I jolt, gasping for air. It's too much. I want more. He does it again.

His tongue lashes and swirls against my clit, slowly at first, then faster and more firmly. I squirm and shake, my hips rocking against his face in time with his movements as he licks me faster, settling into a sharp, demanding rhythm. My nails dig into the bedclothes as my mind goes blank with pleasure.

I writhe on the bed, pinned down by my thighs, his head between my legs, his tongue lashing at my aching clit mercilessly. I hear my desperate gasps and barely manage to muffle them against a pillow as they turn to cries.

Every movement of his tongue against my clit feels better than the last; I hear my cries grow throaty and hoarse and take on a pleading note. *I need it ... I need ...*

But I don't climax. He doesn't let me. He drives me up onto a high of pleasure, making me crave more, but eases off his lashing tongue whenever my muscles start tightening.

Then—brutally, cruelly, brilliantly—he leaves me there, trembling on the edge, as he straightens and reaches into the nightstand to retrieve a condom. He stretches it over his girth and unrolls it as far as it will go, the dark latex not quite reaching the trimmed base. I stare at him, hazy, feverish, hungry ... no longer scared at all.

When he reaches for me, I slide forward into his arms again, offering my neck, my breasts, silently begging for more. Then I feel his mouth and hands start caressing me again, and my mind drifts off on waves of bliss.

I don't know how many minutes pass before he finally enters me; my mind is swimming as he pulls me up onto his massive thighs. His cock presses against my belly, throbbing hard, before he grips my ass and lifts me. When I feel his condom-wrapped head stretch me open, I'm so impatient that I squirm and wrap my legs around him, pulling him deeper into me as he thrusts upward.

"O—oh!" His back arches and his head falls back. I catch his reflection in the mirror and see him go rigid, lips parted and eyes closed with bliss. His chest heaves. "God, baby, you feel so fucking good," he groans, and digs his fingers firmly into the muscle of my ass as he slowly thrusts.

I croon wordlessly, so wild with pleasure from all his caresses that I can't even speak any more. Any pain from being stretched so fully, so quickly, floats away as his hips work me. My hands run up and down his sides, over his back, fingers digging in whenever he thrusts deep. His slow, gentle rhythm builds gradually, even as he shakes and pants from his efforts to restrain himself.

It's amazing how his whole body trembles with pleasure, every powerful muscle tight under my fingers. One shimmy of my hips and he goes rigid, letting out a hoarse little shout, and thrusts faster. He's powerful ... but right now, I have just as much power over him.

His hips buck and he shudders hard as I do it again. "Nnnh. Don't, baby, you feel too good. Let's take care of you first." And he bends his head to take one of my nipples into his mouth again.

I moan, burying my fingers in his hair as he suckles roughly. My clit aches for more stimulation and I grind against him instinctively, unsatisfied yet still awash in pleasure. He shudders and pants and then grips my hips gently to control my movements.

This big, tough gangster is so tender with me, and he wants me so badly. And I know, feeling a rush that drives me even wilder, that I can make him scream if I want.

But right now, my clit aches and my pussy is so tight around him that it makes my legs shake. The sense of teetering on a precipice fills me—but I have no idea what the fall will feel like. I arch my back, sobbing incoherently, my tone pleading again.

Then I feel his hand, warm and smooth, sliding between us, and his fingers exploring my folds just above his thrusting cock. I gasp, bucking against him, as they graze closer and closer to my clit. He draws a shuddering breath through his nose and then, finally, finds the right spot with his fingertips.

I go rigid, and then start rocking my hips in time to his swirling fingertips, heat spilling up my belly, my muscles pulling tighter and tighter.

He hisses through his teeth and thrusts faster, meeting my rhythm as the dual pleasure from nipple and clit builds in my body. I ride his thighs roughly, and he clutches me tighter, somehow able to keep his fingers moving against me as he groans against my skin with each breath.

Every movement of his fingers against my clit feels better; each thrust of his cock drives me closer to the edge. I sob and clutch at him, grinding on him, desperate for more ... and then suddenly, for the first time in my life, it happens.

Pleasure erupts through me, so intense that all I can do is gasp, and tremble, and *feel*. With every wave that hits me, I grind my hips, my voice reduced to breathless sobs.

Suddenly, in the middle of my frenzy, Armand lets go of my nipple and goes rigid, thrusting into me as deep as he can.

His voice rises to low, rumbling shouts as his cock shudders inside me. *Oh. Oh yeah. Oh.* And I cling to him, riding the peak with him, until I collapse into his arms and he relaxes with a contented sigh.

I gasp for air, cradled against his sweaty chest, my first-ever orgasm leaving me slack and tingling. And I'm glad, not just from the pleasure ... but because I waited. I waited for a man I wanted so badly that I finally broke my own rules just for him.

We catch our breath, sweat cooling our bodies in the breeze from the open windows. I hope I wasn't too noisy; I don't hear any movement from Laura's room. That probably means we didn't wake her up.

"Mmm, I need to get rid of this thing." He gently lays me back against the pillows and pulls out of me, gripping the condom at the base of his cock. I feel him leave me and sigh, already missing the feeling of being filled with him.

I watch him walk to the bathroom as I settle into the bed, covers thrown back so I can cool off. My whole body feels ... different. Relaxed, light, my skin tingling. Through half-open eyes, I watch the flex of his back and buttocks as his skin gleams in the moonlight.

He moves into the bathroom and shuts the door. I sigh, stretching out on the broad mattress. I'm completely naked, just sprawled there, shameless, too relaxed to move much. I doze off to the sound of the shower hissing.

I half expect he'll just leave after, but instead he climbs in next to me when he comes back, still naked, hair damp with water. "That was so good, baby," he purrs as he takes me in his arms again. "I haven't busted that hard in years."

I discover I can't speak yet. I gaze at him, overcome, as he bends down and kisses my lips ... then each of my nipples, very softly.

I squirm and moan, shocked by a sudden flare of arousal. "Oh," he notices with a smile. "I think someone might need another orgasm."

"Uh huh," I manage breathlessly. *Oh. Oh yes, please.*

I gasp as he rolls over fluidly to crouch over me. One thigh slides between mine, and he props himself on one hand. The other settles against my tingling pussy again.

"Let's just take care of you then," he murmurs, his voice full of tenderness and deep contentment again. "I want my sweet, brave little Daniela *totally* satisfied. Otherwise, you might not want me back for more."

I always will, I think, enthralled—but then he's caressing me again, and his mouth is tugging softly and insistently at my sensitive nipple. And all I can do is coo and moan softly as he gently, gradually pushes me toward another climax.

This time, it comes almost effortlessly. Ecstasy ripples through me peacefully, slowly, so sweetly that it leaves tears on my cheeks. He kisses them away, and then kisses my lips tenderly.

"Get some sleep," he whispers in my ear as I drift off. "I'll be back later."

I can't wait, I think as I feel him cover me with the silk sheet and then climb off the bed. My frightening evening forgotten, I drift off blissfully.

7

Armand

"What condition is the driver in?" I ask as Tony and I make our way down to the basement. My father has left the interrogation in my hands. I'll have to thank him for that later.

I'm no longer filled with white-hot fury as I walk downstairs. Daniela has seen to that. First she saved my child ... and then she gave me more pleasure than I have felt with a woman in a very long time. And thanks to that—thanks to her—I have my head on straight as I prepare to face the man who tried to take my little girl.

"Well, he got knocked out and he's missing some skin from the rosebushes, but there's nothing broken except maybe his pride. You know she straight up waited until she knew he'd drop far enough that he couldn't get away after? Smart girl you got watching

Laura." Tony shoves his hands in his pockets and looks at me hesitantly.

"What is it, Tony?" I ask patiently as we reach the bottom of the stairs and head down the long hallway that separates the different wings of the sprawling basement. It's brightly lit and white, with a sterile look that clashes with the sumptuous layout upstairs. My mother never goes down here, and as we stop at a steel door halfway down, I'm reminded again of why.

He pauses before opening the door. "You can't kill this guy too soon, Armand. We gotta find out what Frazetti is planning."

"I know," I reply, the picture of cool.

He blinks and spreads his hands. "I don't get it. How can you be so calm?"

"Let's just say that I have ways of burning off my excess energy." And I plan to take advantage of them again as soon as I'm done here. *Sleep well for now, Daniela.* "Besides, you're right. He doesn't die until we extract everything he knows."

Right now, though, this luckless sonovabitch is going to take the place of Carlo and every other goddamned Frazetti who was in on trying to kidnap Laura. He'll be made an example of—because nobody gets to do this to my sweet little girl.

Thank God she never woke up. And thank God Daniela was brave and had a knife handy. But most of all ... thank Daniela, for making sure this fucker couldn't limp away in time to save himself.

I walk into the interrogation room with Tony on my heels, burying every kind and tender part of my personality behind an icy mask. It is time to be the opposite of everything I am with Laura, everything I was just moments ago with Daniela. Fortunately, with this guy, it's easy.

The interrogation room, like the hallway, is designed to be unnerving. The lights are very bright and cover the whole ceiling behind unbreakable panels, the single steel chair is bolted to the floor, and every single surface is white except for the wall-sized two-way mirror. My father and a few others watch behind that panel while I do the dirty work.

I pull my gloves back on as I walk in, staring coldly at the man in the chair. He's battered and dirty, covered in treated scratches, his dark suit torn. He's maybe twenty-five, and stares up at me as I walk toward him, brown eyes blank with fear.

Tony shuts the door and leans against it, folding his arms. I look from Tony's reflection to the man before me, and tilt my head, smirking. "So ... you fucked up."

He starts babbling something about how the others will know what happened when he doesn't show up, and I hold up a finger. "Okay! Ground rules. You speak when spoken to." I reach over, making him cringe, and adjust his lopsided tie over his throat. "Meanwhile, you listen."

I tighten the tie painfully, for emphasis, and then lean back, staring down at him with folded arms. He keeps pulling at the shackles on his arms and legs. *Good luck.* They're welded shut and will have to be cut open with a torch.

"You tried to kidnap my daughter for your boss. That was the plan, right?" The man nods, wide-eyed, and I nod back. "Thought so. Come up the back wall, scoop her out of bed, stuff her in a bag, and suddenly Frazetti has the most valuable hostage."

Another nod. The man gulps, staring up at me. "We weren't gonna hurt her. That wasn't in the plan."

"You mean it wasn't in the part of the plan that Carlo told you." I get right into his face. "But this is the man who murdered his own father to get his position. So the question is ... why do you believe his line of bullshit? Because I sure don't."

I walk around him slowly, the low fury in my voice making him shake and crane his neck around to keep track of me. "You were to take my little girl and blackmail us. And then, Carlo would have killed her to demoralize me, because why the hell not?"

"No!" the man says in genuine shock. "It wasn't nothing like that! He's after you, not the kid!"

He realizes after a moment what he's been goaded

into saying, and I chuckle. "And he's not man enough to confront me directly. He wants to hamstring me by taking my child."

"Look, Mr. Rossini," he swallows, going a shade paler as I stare into his eyes. "I swear I was just doing what the boss told me."

"Of course you were. But that also means you're the kind of man who will take an instruction to kidnap an innocent child from her bed and go through with it." His eyes widen, pupils dilating in fear as I move a hair closer.

"If you want to save your life, I want to know what your boss has planned for us. Every goddamned thing you know."

He stares at me in fear ... and that's when he snaps. But not in the way that I expected.

He gives me a wild grin that shows all his teeth. Maybe he knows he's fucked no matter what he does. Maybe he actually thinks he can intimidate his way out of this or that Frazetti will somehow come rescue him before I put a bullet in his head.

All I know is he starts laughing. Laughing, with tears of terror still streaming down his cheeks. Like he's lost his fucking head.

"You're gonna kill me no matter what I do or say. And Mr. Frazetti will kill me if you don't. You think you can fucking scare me?" he titters, his voice shaking hard the whole time.

I exchange glances with Tony, who gives me a baffled look, then turn back to our tittering prisoner. "Look, how you handle this and how you go out are up to you." I keep my voice firm, refusing to be rattled by his nerves cracking. Interrogations involve emotional strain for everyone involved.

"You're right, you pansy-ass punk. It is in my hands. Or in my mouth, anyway. Fuck you! I ain't telling you nothing!"

Tony and I both lunge forward—I grab the man's head and try and pry my fingers into his mouth as I see him tongue a pill out of his cheek. He bites me, but can't get through the reinforced glove. I struggle with him as he fights to swallow.

He gags suddenly—and I smell a strong scent of bitter almonds. Then Tony is dragging me back away from him as the man goes into convulsions and starts to turn blue. Pink foam froths at the corners of his mouth as that horrible bitter scent gets stronger and stronger.

Tony gets me out as I start coughing and gagging. He slams the door and locks it, then turns to me. "You okay?"

"Some kind of ... cyanide concentrate," I gasp, leaning on the wall. "He swallowed enough to react with his stomach acid and start filling the room with cyanide gas." I only got a whiff of the resulting gas, but it takes me a minute to pull myself together.

The next door down opens and my father walks out, already raising his voice. "What the hell was that? The guy had a poison pill in his cheek? What is this, a fucking spy movie?"

He stomps over to me and grabs me by the shoulders, his manner gruff but worry clear in his eyes. "You all right?"

I nod, wiping my streaming eyes. That horrible smell is gone. "More than a poison pill. He was exhaling poison gas. Guess the plan was to take out his interrogators too. But Tony got me out."

"Yeah, well, that's what I pay him the big bucks for. Hey, Tony! Not bad!" He thumps Tony on the shoulder and congratulates him, stirring morale back up. Drawing attention away from the fact that I lost our subject—and nearly my life.

Fuck.

"First he tries to kidnap my kid and then he has his own guy turn himself into a poison- gas bomb. Carlo's gone from a greedy prick to straight around the bend." My throat is sore. One of the guys gets me a glass of water and I down it greedily.

"Guess we better keep that door sealed until the ventilation system pulls all the poisoned air out. Just glad the lower level has its own circulation or we'd be risking whiffs of that crap getting everywhere." Tony looks between me and my father for confirmation, and we both nod.

"Carlo must be planning something big," my father mutters as we walk off together down the hall. "He left the meeting with a grin on his face. He must have gambled that, either way, we would lose something tonight. But we didn't."

I nod, staying diplomatically quiet. I'm kicking myself for not having the men do a cavity search. I just didn't think it would be necessary. I'll never make that mistake again.

Father heads upstairs to my mother after instructing Tony to keep the guard doubled for the rest of the night. Me, I go up to check on my baby, trying to shake off my disgust and unease at the whole ordeal.

I move into my daughter's room quietly, glad as hell that she's a heavy sleeper. She's still quietly snoozing as I steal over to her bed. One day, I'll tell her what happened. But right now, I'm glad as hell that she doesn't know how close she came to being in the middle of a nasty firefight to save her from kidnapping.

Right now, she's safe. I bend down and kiss her plump little cheek. She stirs and stretches, opening her eyes.

"Hi, Daddy," she murmurs sleepily, and smiles up at me. "Is it time to get up?"

I muffle a cough in my fist. My throat is still a little raw. "No, I'm just coming to check on you before I go to bed. You okay?"

She rubs her eye with the back of one small fist and yawns. "Just had funny dreams. Did you guys beat up Spider-Man?"

"Nah, I wouldn't beat up Spider-Man, he's nice. He wouldn't give me a reason." I stroke her hair back from her face. "Get some more sleep, cutie. Tomorrow we're gonna show the new nanny around."

"I like Daniela. Can we keep her?" She closes her eyes and rolls over.

I smile softly as I think of Daniela ... her new nanny, and my new lover. She saved my child. I'll take care of her financially for the rest of her life, no matter how long she stays.

But I want her to stay. "I hope so," I reply, and brush my fingers over her forehead again before I straighten up to walk away. "I'll be close if you need anything," I say as I slip through the adjoining door.

Daniela's exactly where I left her, fast asleep. I've worn her out. My smile takes on a wicked edge as I stare down at her.

I'm tired, my throat's sore, and I just nearly died.

And my cock's still hardening as I shuck my clothes. Just the sight of her is enough.

I slip into bed behind her and move up close, spooning her and nuzzling her hair.

She stirs and makes a soft sound, rolling toward me and blinking her eyes open. "Thought you left," she says with a sleepy smile.

"I couldn't resist coming back," I murmur in response, kissing her neck softly. The storm inside of me is calming after seeing my daughter. The rest of me needs a distraction. And the sweetness of my new lover's body fits the bill perfectly.

She blushes and lowers her eyes, ridiculously demure for someone wearing nothing but a sheet. "I didn't expect ... any of this." But she doesn't move away, instead nestling against me, her breasts pressing enticingly against my chest.

"I didn't expect you," I murmur, satisfied for the moment to hold her. "But I've got no regrets. Do you?"

"I ... no. I'm just still adjusting. I'm very new at all of this." And suddenly, more blushing.

I blink at her in shock, thinking back to how it felt when I first drove into her. *Holy shit, I'm her first.*

About five million things go through my head at once as I get the guiltiest, hardest boner of my entire life. Am I the first man she's ever been attracted to enough to fuck? Or did I overdo it by seducing her?

Her first. And I can't even love her. A wave of guilt hits me. I don't think my heart can hold another woman after what happened with my wife.

But I can try to treat her right.

I take her chin gently, making her look at me. "If you ever want to stop ... if it bothers you ... let me know. I'll be disappointed, but not angry. This isn't part of your job. If you're not into it, I can't really get into it either. So please, tell me, okay?"

"I will," she promises ... and shyly leans up to kiss me.

The clinging softness of her lips sets me off. I run my hands over her greedily, wanting to learn every inch of her skin. She coos softly under my touch and shivers, her breath growing heavier as her nipples tighten under my fingers. This time, when I kiss her, she melts against me, thighs parting as I roll onto her.

I take my time entering her as she sighs and stretches under me, her hands running soothingly over my skin. Sinking into her warm body, settling into her gentle embrace, I forget every damn problem that is looming over me. She is all there is in my head.

I groan softly in her ear, then whisper, "There we are ... you feel so good. Do you like that?"

She whimpers and shivers as I slide a hand between us to stimulate her. "Oh y—yes ..."

Her warm, slick cunt embraces me again and again

as I slowly roll my hips. My fingers tease her clit gently, working to take her up with me. But she's so excited that I feel her tighten around my shaft right away.

I move inside her slowly, savoring her, ignoring the pounding urge to speed my thrusts and climax. She holds me, cooing gently, sometimes murmuring my name. Warmth washes through me with each reverent whisper.

I know it's risky to let myself get this intense with a woman. I know I'm not thinking straight. But right now, as she starts to pant and tremble, I can't bring myself to care.

I sink into her deep and swirl my fingers over her clit until she gasps and digs her nails into my shoulders. Her head flies back against the pillow and she sobs for air, eyes squeezing closed and face strained with anticipation. Then her back arches, and her muscles spasm around my shaft as she grinds against me.

I start thrusting hard, letting myself go. She whimpers and strains against me as my surging cock sends more contractions through her. I muffle her cries with my mouth, pounding into her slick heat as my balls tighten and my pleasure surges. My muscles tense; she moans and clings to me, hips rising to meet mine.

The orgasm roars through me, so intense it's almost painful, and I hear myself whisper her name. I adore her, she is perfect—I want to keep fucking her for the rest of forever. Then my mind whites out ...

... and when I come back to myself, I'm settled in her arms, cradled so gently, completely spent, and unable to move.

"Oh," I murmur in her ear as I settle my head on her shoulder. I'm struggling to keep my eyelids open. "Oh baby, tell me we can do this again tomorrow."

"I'll be disappointed if we don't," she whispers, still cradling my spent, tingling cock in her warm flesh.

I should get up, I think, even as she unwraps her legs from me and caresses my back gently. She's pulling the sheet up over us as I go limp in her arms. *I really should ...*

My eyes slam closed and I sink into a warm and soothing darkness.

8

Daniela

"Do you like Daddy?" Laura asks me a week later, and I freeze.

"Uh ... what do you mean, sweetie?" Meanwhile I can feel my cheeks burning.

I can't tell this little girl that I've fallen asleep in her daddy's arms every night since moving in, fucked to exhaustion in more ways than I knew existed. I can't tell her that under my high-necked blouse are a dozen purple suck-marks that he's left on my body, or that I'm working up the nerve to use my mouth on his cock.

I wouldn't even tell her any of that if she was over eighteen. That would just be weird.

"He's happy again with you here. He was always quiet before. And he's around more, and that's nice." She gazes at me pleadingly. "So you have to stay, okay?"

I blink in surprise, and then smile at her reassuringly. "I'm not going anywhere. Now did you want to learn more painting?"

The small studio is a converted solarium, like Laura's playroom, and sits on the other side of the hallway. She's got a kid-sized easel set up next to my big one, and she nods enthusiastically and turns her big paper painting pad to the next page.

I'm teaching Laura about secondary colors when the door opens unexpectedly. A tall, stately-looking older woman, her steel-and-silver hair pinned up in braids, breezes in. She looks around the newly-appointed studio before her sharp black eyes fix on me, and then Laura.

"Good morning!" she greets us. She looks me up and down, assessing me for a moment before turning a brilliant smile on Laura. "Hello, sweetheart. How are things going?"

"Grandma! You came down!" Linda jumps up and almost runs over to her with a loaded paintbrush. I deftly nip it from her fingers before she can get near her grandmother's rose Dior suit.

The grandmother shoots me a relieved look this time, and hugs her granddaughter tightly. "There we are." She doesn't bend down, her stance stiff. "How are you doing? I wanted to see how things are working out with your new nanny."

"Oh, Daniela's so nice. She's teaching me colors! Do you want to see?" She takes her grandmother's hand and leads her over to her art pad as I step aside and start cleaning the brush.

I keep an ear turned on them as the two of them chatter away. I know that passing the Grandma Test is part of the job of a live-in nanny. I don't resent her investigating, even if it makes me a little nervous.

Once she's satisfied that Laura is happy with me, the woman leaves her granddaughter to paint some sunny scene with bright houses, and comes to me. I put on a professional smile, and incline my head slightly in respect as she gets close. She pauses at a conversational distance, and then settles in, considering me again.

"I wanted to thank you for very likely saving my granddaughter's life," she says quietly. "Your quick thinking saved her from a frightening night at the least."

"It needed to be done," I reply simply, but firmly. "I was scared, but I couldn't let him go near her." I glance back at Laura, who is engrossed in painting the perfect yellow sun.

"Now that's what I like to see." She lifts her chin approvingly and raises her voice back to conversation level. "And Laura adores you as well. How are you getting on after such an ... eventful first week?"

"It's been nice and quiet since the, um, incident, so I'm fine. It takes some getting used to, especially with all the security."

Aside from shopping for new belongings on Armand's dime and retrieving my art supplies from campus, I haven't left the grounds all week. But every single time, I went with someone armed.

She nods and smiles faintly. "You're a nice girl. I wouldn't blame you if you found all this a little scary. I just don't want to think that anything happening around here would scare you off."

"No, I, um ... I've lived in some pretty bad neighborhoods. Compared to that, this is nice. Pretty, clean, and usually safe and quiet." My smile's a bit awkward.

She's still pinning me with her gaze, like she can see into my head. For some reason my attention goes right to the tiny, faintly sore spot beside my areola where Armand's mouth left a delicate love-bite, and a slight blush creeps over my cheeks.

Do not think about sex with Armand in front of his mother.

"And my son? How is he treating you?" And her gaze pierces me again.

"He's been pretty good to me, especially since that night." My mouth is like a desert suddenly, and my heart is beating too fast. *What does she know?* "Is something wrong?"

"Well ... it's just that you should know something. My son has a tendency to ..." she lowers her voice again. "... flirt with the childcare staff."

Her eyes search my face and my mouth goes dry. Her son's been all over me every night; he's left marks on me that I treasure but am terrified of anyone seeing. Other than that, he's simply friendly, and takes good care of my material needs.

I don't know if our relationship will ever deepen past friends with benefits. I'm having too much fun right now to feel too bad about it ... but I doubt his mother would ever understand that. And my blush right now feels like it could light up the room.

"Flirted, yes, but nothing creepy, if that's what you're worried about. If he ever had that habit, he's broken himself of it." I smile reassuringly ... but she doesn't look convinced.

"Sweetheart, I'm telling you this for your own good. Armand isn't a bad person, but he's irresponsible in certain ways. I'm not worried about his being creepy or coercive with you." Her voice stays low, and she smiles sadly. "I just don't want him breaking your heart."

I blink at her, surprised. "Oh. So that's ... been a problem?"

"Four nannies in sixteen months, honey," she sighs. "He's like a kid in a candy store. They fall for him, but he's not over his wife, so they leave."

Her gaze becomes piercing again. "I don't want Laura to lose you because my son is ... my son. So ... I'm concerned."

Oh boy. This has suddenly gotten complicated. "Yes, ma'am, I understand. I'll do my best to help keep things around here drama-free. And as I said to Laura, I'm not going anywhere."

She stares at me a moment longer, then nods once. "Good. Just wanted to make sure."

But as she goes back to playing with her granddaughter, I feel my first stirrings of doubt. And after she leaves and Laura goes down for her nap, I go back to my room and open the bedside drawer.

The bedside drawer that has been stocked with condoms and lube since before I moved in. Ready for the next pretty young nanny that Armand hired.

Like a kid in a candy store.

I swallow, feeling uneasy—then sigh and walk to the window, hands in my hair. *This shouldn't bother me. So what if he has a thing for women who are good with his daughter?*

But being one in a string of them who had to leave because they fell for him and he didn't reciprocate? That feels weird. How special am I to him, really?

And will he really stop pursuing me for sex if the knowledge that there's no love between us hurts too much and I have to stop?

I set my jaw. I have to be realistic about this. He's my boss and my sex partner, not my boyfriend. And he's been honest with me—about everything but my predecessors, anyway.

But as far as I'm concerned, we still have to have a serious talk.

Twenty minutes later, I hear a tap on the adjoining door and brace myself. He doesn't visit me for sex during naptime; he probably has something to talk about. Maybe the same thing I do.

He steps inside and immediately I see the wild hunger in his eyes and lose all my nerve to confront him. Instead, I'm suddenly fighting a volcanic surge of desire. Maybe it's the novelty, or the risk, or the fact that he interrupted his day out of sheer need for me—but all it takes is that look to set me off.

I want to ask him about his mother's warning. I want to ask him about the condoms in the bed stand. But instead we fly together, stripping off our clothes impatiently then tangling up, hands and mouths all over each other.

"I need you," he growls hoarsely against my lips. "I need you now."

Instead of confronting him, I shove the thought aside in a fit of naughty rebellion, suddenly resenting having Armand's mother's nose in our business. Instead of asking about the well-stocked drawer of condoms from before I moved in, I help him roll one on. Instead of backing off in worry, I push further, ending up on my hands and knees as he covers me from behind.

"I can't get enough of you," he whispers against the back of my neck—and then arches and lets out a grunt of satisfaction as his cock head pushes firmly into me. "Oh. Oh yes, baby."

His cock slides into my slick, aching pussy from an angle I've never felt before and I groan, rolling my ass against his loins as he grabs my hips and starts to thrust. "Do it, do it, do it," I whisper as he speeds up, his sounds of pleasure going deeper and hoarser as we make the bedsprings creak.

His hand reaches around to my front and grips my pussy firmly. He starts to knead in time with his thrusts, and I tighten around him and shimmy harder, feeling my body start to ramp up to orgasm. "Oh yes ... yes, just like that ..." I gasp softly.

I feel like I'm floating on a hot tide, aching from nipples to knees with sexual need as his hips slap against my ass again and again. I arch my back, grinding against him hard as his fingers bring me to the brink.

"Oh!" His shout sets me off; I bite my lip and muffle my cries as ecstasy makes me squirm. Each long roll of my hips gets another sharp shout out of him. He pounds into me briefly—and then groans against the back of my neck as I feel the climax make his cock shake.

Somehow he manages to catch me before I collapse on my face. I feel him panting hard for air against me, each breath pushing his still-firm cock into me and setting off fresh ripples of pleasure.

"Oh God," he gasps. "The best. The fucking *best*." And he brushes my hair aside and kisses the back of my neck.

I settle onto the bed and roll onto my side with him spooned behind me, his cock still half inside. He doesn't seem to want to let me go; instead he nuzzles my hair and kisses my shoulders, murmuring in my ear. "Did you like that?"

It takes me a few moments to catch my breath. As I do, my eyes focus on the half-open bed-stand drawer with its huge supply of condoms and lube. *Stocked up ... like he just expected he would be fucking whoever took the job.*

Then I smile a little at the irony. *Well ... he wasn't wrong. But still ...*

I'm still left wondering, even as I lie in his arms with my body tingling from climax, if he means it when he says sex with me is really the best. *Or did he say the same thing to the last nanny he fucked to distraction in this bed?*

"Oh yes," I purr reassuringly, but a twinge goes through my heart. And suddenly I'm too confused inside to bring up what's bothering me.

I let my eyes close instead, and pretend to be napping until he kisses my temple and slips away. "Get some rest, *cara mia*," he murmurs sleepily in my ear. "You'll need your strength for tonight."

And damn him ... despite my nagging doubts, I still can't wait.

9

Armand

"You're fucking her, aren't you?" Gina asks bluntly as soon as the door to her office is closed. "Your mother knows."

I sigh as I slip into the chair across the desk from her. "Well, good morning to you too."

"I'm quite serious, Armand. There's trouble brewing, and we need you focused." She has her glasses off and is massaging the bridge of her nose. Bad sign—it's her habitual gesture when dealing with idiots.

"Are you suggesting that I can't focus if I'm getting laid regularly?" I try to sound amused, but in reality I'm annoyed as hell. My mother is a nosy hen about certain things, and it's always been awkward that my romantic life is somehow one of them.

It just rubs salt in the wound that Gina's on her side.

Gina rolls her eyes. "Armand. I'm not saying any such thing. I'm saying that you have a pattern. You go through a honeymoon period with these girls, and then they fall for you, and then they leave because they can't stand to see you every day when you don't love them back."

I start to speak, but she quickly cuts in. "Daniela's only been with us a month, and she's the best we've gotten in quite a while. Your mother has said it and now I'm saying it: she's good for Laura. Can you just ... avoid emotionally devastating her and driving her away?"

"I don't want to hurt her," I say quickly, and so sharply that it surprises me. Maybe it shouldn't. I've spent hours in Daniela's bed each day—in her bed, in her shower, on her floor ... and twice, when Laura was out with her grandparents, in my own giant, luxurious bed down the hall.

I don't want to give her up either. The sex is so incredible that it takes me back to my honeymoon. None of the other women I've been with since Bella can compare to her. Not even the most talented call girl.

But I can't get enough of this. I have to have her every time Laura is asleep or away and I can get Daniela alone. In her arms, I can rest.

In her arms, I can forget that I'm a widower for a while, and simply be a man.

Gina has stopped her lecturing and calmed a little, and as I come back to myself, I see she is peering at me wryly. "You've got a bit of a dreamy look on your face there, boss."

I cough into my fist and then hide my consternation in a swallow of coffee. "I'm not sure what you mean."

"Nothing. You just seem ... more attached to this one, somehow. Almost protective." That look in her eyes is too piercing ... and way too amused. "How special is she to you?"

In another life, if I could love again, I'd fucking marry her. "She saved my daughter's life. Of course she's special," I grumble defensively.

Her eyebrow rises, and to my surprise, she relaxes and sits back. "You know what? I think I'll just see where things go with the two of you. As long as you don't make her so unhappy that she leaves, Armand."

I nod at her, feeling both relieved and embarrassed. "And my mother?"

"Oh, I really wouldn't advise discussing any of this with her. Just keep things quieter. You've been noticeably eager to end your afternoon meetings at Laura's naptime, and then you mysteriously vanish for an hour."

Oh. Shit. I'd hoped no one would notice that.

I lick my lips. "I'll take it under advisement. So what about the Frazettis?"

"Carlo keeps asking if we've seen his driver or his car. We still have them on ice. Keeping him guessing about the guy's fate was a good idea. Your father's impressed.

Rattling Carlo by leaving him to wonder how much we know about the attempted kidnapping has apparently distracted him from his warpath some." She hands me another of her folders.

"However, he killed two more small-timers in the Bronx. Your father reminded him that he didn't have the authority to sanction anyone in our territory, but Carlo ..." She gives me a thin smile.

"Bluster and vague threats?" I sigh, opening the folder. The two drug dealers' autopsy reports and associated police reports seem completely straightforward. One thing angers me especially, though.

"Fuck, one of these dealers was just an overambitious kid. Sixteen!" I let out a sigh. *Without my family name to protect me, that could have been me.*

"Track down his family, send them a blind transfer of fifty thousand, and pay off their debts." I check the other casualty—a complete prick with a record as long as my arm, most of it violent. "This one can rot."

"You're talking more like a Don every day," Gina says proudly.

Keeping our cards close to our chests even after such an outrage is the best idea I've had in a while—good enough to even get Father's approval on. I want blood for what almost happened to my daughter—and to me. But so far, with Laura safe and Daniela to make love to, I've managed to avoid doing anything impulsive.

That's what they want anyway, I think as I go up to my office to get a look at all the collected data on the Frazettis's new murder and conquest hobby. *They want to make us—to make me—do something reckless so they can take me out.*

I'm not about to let that happen.

I spend some time with Laura before bed, reading to her in Daniela's place, letting Daniela take a break before I pounce on her again. I've been trying to spend more time with my daughter since the night I almost lost her. And she notices.

"Daddy, could you marry Daniela for me?" she asks out of nowhere, and I almost drop the copy of *The Hobbit* that I'm reading from. I blink at her, and she continues earnestly, "She's really nice, and you're happy now."

I stare at her in amazement. "Uh ... well ... I ..." *Shit.*

How to tell her that I'm not over her mom, that I can never really be over her mom?

Just thinking about marrying Daniela sends a wave of guilt and self-reproach through me. *She deserves better than a marriage without love.*

My mother would love it. She wants me to have a wife so I look more mature to those we deal with. Daniela's Italian, Catholic, from a family connected to ours—she was even a virgin before me. She's perfect.

But she's not Bella.

Laura is staring at me expectantly. I lean over and kiss her forehead. "That's going to take some thinking about."

Once she's in bed and asleep, I go through the side door to visit Daniela—and stop short a moment, staring, before stepping in and pulling the door closed. "You ... went shopping again," I breathe almost reverently, the day's problems forgotten.

Her demure bra and panty sets are sexy enough, clinging to her curves as they do, but the filmy silk camisole that's the same blue as her eyes is on another level. I can just see hints of the matching panties beneath it. As she moves toward me, eyes still shy but a soft heat in their depths, I feel my cock go so hard that it hurts.

"I would do anything to fuck you right now," I murmur as she moves forward to kiss me. My arms start to slide around her ... and then she startles me completely by sliding to her knees in front of me.

"Take off your clothes, then, and stand still." The command still has a hint of shyness, but that only turns me on more. She's being bold to please me. I can't remember the last time a woman did that for me without being paid.

I strip obediently and stand there as she very gently takes my cock between her slim fingers. *Oh God.* My chest heaves, hands flexing at my sides as she starts to caress me.

Her small, soft hands explore every inch of my cock, stroking the head, the shaft, softly cupping my balls. I bite my lip hard and force myself to hold still and let her play. She's shy, normally; this is a hell of a nice surprise, especially on top of the lingerie.

She leans forward a little as she strokes me, and I feel her warm breath on the head of my cock. "Daniela," I gasp.

Then she kisses my cock head, so softly, and then again. The warm, slick little tip of her tongue darts out and starts exploring me, stroking back and forth over the taut skin until a shudder goes through me with every little swipe.

Her hands circle my shaft softly ... and then her lips engulf the head of my cock and I groan through my teeth. She takes in more of me, careful with her teeth, her small, hot mouth sliding over my cock slowly. When she starts to suckle and lick me, my eyes roll closed and I have to fight hard to stay standing.

Her long, loving tastes leave me panting for air. Her struggle to take in more—to please me more—makes my chest ache with its sweetness. *Oh, you darling, amazing woman ...*

Drunk with pleasure, I arch my back, hips strained, balls tight to my body, groaning as she runs her tongue up and down my length. "Oh, you're so good at that, baby. Anything you want ... ever ... just don't stop ..."

She doesn't, even as she gasps for air through her nostrils and struggles to keep her head moving. And finally, I can't take it anymore, and grab her shoulders to stop her.

I gently withdraw my throbbing cock from her mouth, and scoop her off her knees and into my arms. She goes willingly, shivering and clinging to me. I lay her back on the edge of her bed and pull off her panties, barely avoiding tearing them.

Then I pull her hips to the very edge and thrust into her. She's so hot and slick that my cock goes in at once—and the thought that she got so wet just from sucking my cock makes it feel better than ever.

"Oh yes!" she's sobbing as I start fucking her hard enough to shake the bed. *"Yes!"*

I pound into her, relishing the feel of her muscles

tightening around me, and the oily softness of her welcoming cunt. She's incredibly turned on, barely needing any fingering before she's bucking under me and digging her nails into my back.

Her hips grind sweetly against mine, faster and faster as I thrust in hard. Then she presses up against me, crying out and sobbing for air—and I feel her contractions caress my shaft.

I sink in deep one last time and empty myself into her. It's so good that I barely bite back a scream.

Oh yes. Yes. Daniela...

The climax drops me like a hammer blow.

I open my eyes and realize I've collapsed over her at the edge of the bed. I barely have the strength to climb off of her. I lie there tingling, head hazy. As she cuddles against me, I close my eyes and drift off, feeling more content than I can ever remember feeling.

10

Daniela

When I wake up in Armand's arms, I know that I'm in trouble. I'm warm and safe, filled with deep comfort, my head pillowed against his shoulder as he breathes softly. In the pre-dawn dimness I can see his naked skin gleaming, his curls damp and wild.

His face is so peaceful. I gaze up at him ... and I feel it again. That same nagging pang of longing and regret that I have to keep shoving aside when I'm with him.

He doesn't love me. The most he can be to me is a friend with benefits. He's told me about his wife's death. How recently it was, how hard he has been affected by it.

He's been completely honest with me. He's amazing in bed, and he's kind. That's all I can expect.

I can't afford to fall in love with him. Things are lovely as they are. *Expecting more is expecting too much.*

But then why are there tears in my eyes?

I tuck my head under his chin and he grunts in his sleep, his grip on me tightening protectively. I close my eyes, heart aching, and realize it's too damn late. I've already fallen for him.

That is the last thing I should have done. God, why are emotions so stupid sometimes? I guess I'll have to keep it to myself.

For now, at least, I have the warmth and softness of these stolen moments. And the tender way he treats me, even in his sleep. He may never be able to love again after the death of his wife, but ... some people marry and still don't get to feel this good.

Mom and Dad's marriage was proof enough of that. My early memories of living with them in that small, shabby apartment involve a lot of yelling. Not fists flying or plates thrown, but drama and bellowing that made my ears and heart hurt.

Arguing over money, over what I realize now was their nonexistent sex life, about Dad's unemployment, about Mom's stress drinking. They bickered about everything, including me. It never really stopped. When they didn't have anything real to fight about, they bickered over tiny things: toilet rolls that weren't replaced, neglected chores, disagreements over TV shows.

In public, at family gatherings, at my school, on holidays, they never stopped fighting and sniping at each other. They bickered their way through car rides, with Dad getting angry and sometimes driving recklessly, terrifying me. And one day, fortunately when I wasn't in the car, they decided to get into their last bitter fight, probably over nothing, while on a winding mountain road.

They were so distracted by whatever they were blowing up over on that sunny afternoon that the skid marks from braking started only ten feet from the safety barrier. Even in the midst of my tears over losing them, part of me wondered if they argued the entire way down, with only the impact silencing them.

Those two each wanted more from the other than they were willing to give. They weren't satisfied with each other and instead of settling or walking away, they attacked each other over it endlessly. And so they were both doubly miserable.

I look up at Armand again. He'd already told me how much he is willing to give me. He was very honest. I can't be angry at him for doing exactly what he said he would do.

I won't make the same mistake my parents did. I'll learn to deal with reality instead, even if it makes me sad some-

times. It hurts to fully understand that I love Armand and know that he can't do the same, not just in the abstract, but in my life, in my heart, right now.

But my life is still better than it's ever been ... and what I have with Armand is still better than what my parents had. I can make myself deal with it ... somehow. And so I fall asleep in Armand's arms again, peacefully, even with tears on my cheeks.

When I wake up again, he's gone. I swallow my disappointment and get up to get ready for work.

We fall into a routine after the fifth week or so—a routine that is anything *but* routine. In the mornings, after some time to myself, I have breakfast with Laura and take a walk with her around the grounds. Then it's time for lessons. She's a smart little girl and she's learning to read incredibly fast.

Then comes lunchtime. Painting lessons. Another walk. Her nap. And then ...

Then Armand slips into my room for the first time for the day.

Sometimes, in the late afternoons, Laura's grandparents or her father take her somewhere, and then I have time for errands or for finishing my own paintings. I'm doing more work now than I was able to do in school. Armand talks about renting out a gallery for me for a showing.

The weeks roll past quickly and late summer sets

in. Laura is happy and sleeps quietly, safe. She's become an avid painter, and she's learning that fast too. I've finished four paintings myself—all fantasy landscapes in bright colors.

Except for the tight security and the strange, tense meetings that sometimes take place on the first floor, I can almost forget that I'm working for mobsters. They might be any wealthy, eccentric family who worry about security and adore their granddaughter.

Armand has gotten every single window screen in the house replaced with security mesh and titanium frames that lock from the inside. They look almost identical to the old ones. The result is much prettier than the security bars I used to look through at Nonna's house.

Sometimes, alone in the mornings, as I wake to an empty bed, I wonder about Nonna's old house. I keep being tempted to check and see if it ever actually sold to anyone, or if the bank finally gave up on her dilapidated bungalow and tore it down.

I even bring it up to Armand once, when he catches me brooding one morning. But I still can't bring myself to go find out. It reminds me of that night I was thrown out by police for no reason, and my anger then might tempt me to ask my new employers to … intervene.

And that's a path I can't ever go down. So I put it all

out of my mind. *I have a home. I'm safe. I don't need revenge.*

By the end of August, however, something else has started nagging at me more than I can possibly just ignore. In fact, it's really got me worried.

I'm starting to feel queasy whenever I have anything to eat, especially in the mornings. Worse, my tastes are suddenly changing. Melted cheese, that Italian-American ambrosia, now makes me sick to my stomach. I've gotten so sensitive to alcohol that I can't even handle cough syrup.

I also haven't had a period in two months.

I can't be pregnant. We've been careful. Sure, we've been screwing like rabbits, but we always use condoms.

Don't we? I catch myself wracking my brain one afternoon, after barely keeping down a sandwich. I can't remember a single act of lovemaking that didn't involve a condom, at least when he was inside me.

But we're always so frenzied together ... as if we're drunk on each other. Could we have forgotten? All it takes is one time.

I've never been with anyone else. If I'm pregnant, it's Armand's. I can't hide that fact.

But what in the world am I going to tell him if I am? And how is he going to react?

It's like asking about the condoms, and about how

special I am to him. No matter how determined I am to speak to him about it, whenever I see him next, and every time after that, the words stick in my throat, and I throw myself into his arms to distract myself from this growing, secret terror.

11

Armand

I keep falling asleep in Daniela's room and having to slip back to my own when I finally wake up. I don't love having to do the walk of shame in my own house, hours before anyone but the guard shift is up. I keep barely avoiding running into one of my men, thanks to the doubled guard.

I know I shouldn't stick around too long after we make love. Lingering and cuddling with Daniela, sleeping with her in her bed ... both of those things run the risk of sending her mixed messages. I don't want her to flee because of a broken heart.

And not just because Laura, my mother, Gina, and probably even Tony will all give me hell for it. But because ... if she goes, I'll miss her.

I keep trying to get myself out of her bed, showered, dressed, and headed to my own room as soon as I get rid of the condom. But half the time, I keep giving in to the temptation to just come back to bed for a while.

To hold her. To watch her sleep. Sometimes, to wake up to warm, sleepy seconds in the dead of the night.

The urge to stay is just too great sometimes, and that's dangerous. But it's not actually the hardest part of my relationship with Daniela.

The hardest part of my relationship with Daniela is hiding it from my mother. She means well, and so I can't resent her nosiness too much—but sometimes she treats me as if I'm still a damn kid. And the way she checks up on me by asking my daughter is dirty pool.

But this morning, she blindsides me completely. "Daniela's looking a bit pale these days, isn't she?" she asks in the mildest of tones over breakfast. "Especially in the mornings."

I nearly choke on a bite of omelet. It takes everything I have to keep a straight face as I swallow. *Shit. What is Mother talking about? What is it that she's seen that I haven't?*

My mother just stares at me knowingly.

A terrible suspicion creeps into my head. *Oh God. Wait. No. Fuck.*

It's been about two and a half months since I took

Daniela as my lover. Time enough for morning sickness to start ... if that's what it is. *But how can that be? I always use a damn condom, and I've never noticed one break!*

My mother still watches me silently. I blink back at her and say in nearly honest confusion, "I hadn't noticed. I'll ask her about it."

"You do that," she replies in an arch tone, and I feel the hair on the back of my neck stand up.

Shit. Daniela, what aren't you telling me? I know she's not seeing anyone else. Hell, I haven't even wanted anyone else since we first fucked either. Anyway, if there's a kid, I know it's mine. So why not tell me?

Unless, of course, she just has no idea how to bring it up. Or is she scared that I'll get angry?

I hold out through the rest of the meal and a meeting with my dad, where he complains about having to wear his bulletproof vest in this heat. I beg him to either do that or use one of the armored suits I bought for him. He's complaining, complaining ... but I know that Carlo must want him as dead as he wants me.

"Father, come on. I know you hate wearing body armor. But you can't just walk around on the street without it. Not with Carlo gearing up for war."

"You want to tell me what good it's gonna do me to have a vest to protect me from bullets if I end up having a heart attack from the heat because of it?" he grumbles, and waves a hand when I try to reason with him.

I carry that frustration under wraps for the rest of the afternoon, as I'm stuck in back-to-back meetings. I'm carrying the worry about Daniela, too. If she's pregnant ... and it's mine ... I have to look after her.

We're both Catholic. Getting rid of it won't sit well with either of us. *I could marry her. That would satisfy my mother, and give the kid a father.*

It's a surprisingly pleasant option. At least I wouldn't have to sneak around like a rebellious teenager when it came to my sex life anymore. I also wouldn't have a bastard, and Daniela would be taken care of properly.

But how is that fair to her? She's a great girl. She deserves to marry a man who can love her, not my battle-scarred widower ass.

Finally, after my insane day, I have dinner with Daniela and my daughter. Laura wants chicken fingers and fries again, and Daniela compromises by adding a big salad and fruit for dessert. I watch happily—no matter what other weird crap is going on, she's so damn good with my little girl.

But she also eats lightly, and oddly. Pasta with no cheese. Avocado but no romaine. She takes the skin off her chicken and barely eats half of it.

She looks so sick that, once dinner is over, I tell her I'll take care of Laura for a few hours, and ask her to take care of herself. She blushes, but nods thankfully and hugs Laura good night. The soft, longing look she gives me before retreating back upstairs hits me right in the heart.

God, I wish I could love you.

I'm doing better with Laura, mostly from watching Daniela with her. Before we go to bed, I help her proudly mount the stairs to present my mother and father with a painting of bunnies. Father grins wider than he has since he had to quit cigars, and Mother praises her and calls a maid to get it framed and hung right away.

Not too bad, Rossini, I think once I've gotten Laura ready for bed and read to her until she falls asleep. *You might actually get the hang of this dad thing.*

But then I go to check on Daniela—and find her in the bathroom, collapsed over the toilet, sobbing.

12

Daniela

It's really hard to buy a pregnancy test when you constantly have large, protective, overly curious men following you around. I only managed it because I headed deep into the no-man's land of feminine hygiene products at the drugstore and grabbed one off an end cap while getting some tampons. My guard didn't even want to look at the box—or the test tucked behind it—when it was being rung up.

But now, after throwing up my dinner, I've finally worked up the nerve to take it … and now I'm staring one of my worst fears in the face. *Pregnant.*

Armand, who can't love me, has gotten me pregnant.

There's nothing to stop him from throwing me out to cover his own ass. There's nothing keeping him from making me homeless and hopeless right now, just like the bank did. *It's all over ... and it's not even my fault. But I bet he'll blame me!*

The upset sets my stomach off again. Once I flush the toilet, I toss the test aside on the sink and sob helplessly, my legs too weak to support me.

The sound of the side door opening just makes me cry harder. I can't escape from this confrontation now, or whatever comes after it. And I don't know if I can handle that.

I hear him walk toward me. His clothes rustle as he moves into the bathroom—and pauses. I hear the click of him lifting the pregnancy test to examine it.

I close my eyes, my sobs drying up as an icy knot takes over my stomach.

"So you just found out yourself for sure." To my utter shock, he actually sounds relieved. "Were you ... gonna say something to me?"

For the first time ever, he seems uncertain. Maybe even a little vulnerable. And my heart goes out to him —and weirdly, that helps. "Of course. It's yours. I've never wanted anybody else enough to sleep with them."

He winces, his eyes closing in what looks like shame. And I start sobbing again, hiding my face, realizing that I really am just like all those other girls that came before me—sentimental, stupid, and way too trusting.

"Okay, okay. Come on, baby, it's all right. Don't cry." He wraps his arms around me from behind, and pulls me backward onto his lap.

I gulp and sniffle like a kid. "Y—you said I couldn't expect anything besides friends with benefits, and I—I never did. I was doing okay! But now I'm pregnant, and I don't know what to do!"

He hugs me and strokes my damp hair back. "No, no, come on now. The damn condom failed. You didn't. What the fuck would I blame you for?"

I turn partway and blink up at him. His face blurs and then comes back into focus. He's smiling. "You're not mad?"

"Not at you," he sighs in response. "I fucked up. I should have gotten the snip after the funeral, like I wanted."

"What should I do?" I whisper, feeling my first thin trickle of hope. *He doesn't hate me. He's not talking like he's going to throw me out.*

"Take care of yourself and our baby, and keep quiet for now. I'll take you out to a doctor tomorrow, have them confirm and run some tests." His hand moves through my hair soothingly. "It's okay, sweetheart. We're gonna work this out."

I manage to smile through my tears. The relief I

feel inside is tentative, but it's there. He might not love me ... but he's not abandoning me either.

"It's a girl," the dapper, aging Dr. Greene tells me proudly, her full lips curving into a dazzling smile. "You're between eight and nine weeks, completely healthy, and so is the baby."

Sitting beside me as I sit on the exam table, Armand squeezes my hand. "You hear that, sweetheart? You're doing good."

I smile back at him, wrestling with my mixed feelings. I've always wanted to be a mother ... but I was thinking of my late twenties as a good time for that. Not now.

And I definitely didn't want to be having a kid outside of wedlock, or let someone who didn't love me get me pregnant. I wanted to be married, and stable, and all right. But none of that has happened.

Armand happened instead. And now a baby has happened. And I just have to deal with it all.

"You okay?" he asks in the car as we're driving back.

"I don't know," I say honestly. "You know we're not gonna be able to hide this forever. It's not like you can send me away without it affecting Laura."

"That's too true," he sighs. "But what we can do is

keep it quiet for a few months while we figure out what to do."

I bite my lip and nod. It's not an ideal answer. It will only cover us for a few months. I'm naturally curvy, with a bit of a belly, but eventually I'm going to start showing.

I have no idea what we'll do then. But at least Armand isn't abandoning me.

I change my diet to deal with the morning sickness, cutting out a lot of fats and letting my weird new appetites dictate what I eat. It helps, and within a week or so I'm no longer having to sneak off to the bathroom. Except for a few comments about being a picky eater, nobody seems to notice.

Armand and I still make love every night, but I'm starting to need naps in the afternoon. Once or twice, I wake up in his arms anyway, sex or no sex. It confuses me and comforts me at the same time, leaving me wondering again where I stand with him.

It's getting harder not to tell him that I love him, too.

I try not to resent him for what he can't give me. I try not to let it make me depressed. I'm determined to see this through.

After all, whether I like it or not, pretty soon there will be two kids around here that need me.

13

Armand

I'm keeping a big secret now, to keep the peace while I figure out what to do. If my mother knows I've fathered a bastard, she'll probably literally explode. Maybe I deserve that—but the fallout could reach Daniela or Laura, and that can't happen.

For a few weeks after that first visit to the doctor, the deception works. Daniela is less sick, she's taking care of herself, and my mother has stopped asking awkward questions. I still don't know how we're going to handle this long-term, but I'm confident that, given enough time, we'll figure something out.

Then, one sleepy evening in mid-September, the roof falls in.

I'm with Daniela in Laura's bedroom, the two of us

reading Laura a bedtime story, when I hear running and shouting in the hallways. They both look up at me in alarm as I stand. "Stay here and try to stay calm," I order before slipping out the door.

Tony meets me in the hallway and we turn to hurry toward the lobby. "What the hell is going on?" I demand. "Is it an attack?"

"Don't know. The gate guards called me up, freaking out. Whatever it is, it happened just outside." We reach the stairs and take them two at a time as our men join us from the side hallways. My heart is pounding hard; I don't know whether to draw my gun.

Then I get in view of the foyer and my heart drops into my shoes.

My mother is standing in the doorway, very still, her best fur stole and purple opera dress spattered with blood. There's a look in her eyes I've never seen before: wide, lost, glazed with tears. She catches sight of me and her shoulders shake, but she still just ... stands there as I hurry up to her.

They were coming back from an early showing of Chicago. *Where's my father? Was it a car accident? What the hell is going on?*

"Mother?" I stop short in front of her and look her over worriedly. "Are you hurt?"

She shakes her head, her eyes brimming over. She

has her rosary looped around both hands and blood in her braids. *Not her blood.*

"It's your father," she says in a shaky voice. "You were right. He should have worn a vest …"

Oh God, I think. And then she's toppling forward, eyes rolling closed, and I leap to catch her.

"It was an ambush," Tony says to me twenty minutes later. "Definitely Carlo's guys. They killed themselves the same way as the wall climber, to keep from talking, but we got the pill out of one guy's mouth. He's pretty beat up, but he can talk."

I nod. "Prepare a room for him. If he does anything to try and harm himself, drug him."

Carlo has murdered my father. He has murdered my father outside the gates of our own home. He thinks he can do the same to me.

I'm in the same suit as before, smeared with my father's blood, a pistol on the desk in front of me. "So they used snipers right outside our damned gates."

Tony sighs and nods. "That's right."

"And my mother?" I look up at him and he shifts his weight awkwardly.

"Sedated. This hit her real hard. The guy got him right through the heart." He winces when he sees my expression.

At least it was too fast for him to suffer. But Mother …

Carlo is going to pay for this.

I'm numb inside as I scoop my mother off the couch and carry her back to the elevator. She won't want anyone seeing her like this. She's lost her husband—I won't let her lose her dignity too.

I have one of the guards take a message up to Daniela to keep Laura upstairs and calm while I take care of business, promising to join them soon. Then I go to my bedroom suite, wash my father's blood off, and change into my best black suit. Inside of me, rage simmers like a lava pocket.

Ten minutes later, everyone but my immediate family and the current guard assembles in the meeting room. I stand at the head of the table, in my father's place. My back is stiff, and I turn my burning gaze on everyone assembled.

"New Don," I say simply, not needing the nods of acceptance. "New rules. I want every single man or woman who owes allegiance to the Frazettis. When you find one, bag them and stick them in the basement."

"What if they get violent?" Tony asks gravely.

"Then put a bullet in their head, get rid of the gun, and leave." I clench my fists, knuckles pressed against the tabletop. "Either way, I want a message sent. If you work for the Frazettis in any capacity, your days are numbered."

I don't want to just pick off Carlo's men or drive them to quit. I don't want to stay here having meetings. I want to blow up Carlo's penthouse with him inside it.

"We're not going to go take him out, boss?" Tony checks in, seeing my expression.

I shake my head. "No. That is what he's hoping we'll try. He attacked us where we live to try and goad us into trying the same with him. I've got no doubt he's waiting for us over there with all his guys ready and a bunch of nasty surprises."

There's muttering around the table, heads nodding.

"So how will we deal Carlo?"

I look back at Tony briefly and then nod. "He's mine. I'll give a million dollars to the man who brings him to me alive."

I check on my mother before going back to see Laura and Daniela. Her maid has gotten her cleaned up, dressed, and put to bed. She looks strangely shrunken lying there in the grand bed she once shared with my father—as if she's lost more tonight than just her husband.

A million things rush through my head. Anger at Carlo. Anger at my father, who refused to wear any kind of protective clothing in the heat and was shot in the chest because of it.

Anger at myself, for not somehow preventing all of this.

"I'll get this guy, Mother," I promise her quietly before slipping out the door. "Just hold on."

I hesitate before walking into my daughter's room. She loves her grandpa. I'm about to break her sweet little heart, and I can't help it, because telling her is my job.

Then I brace myself, and walk inside.

14

Daniela

It's almost dawn. The small clock on my bed stand ticks away softly in the dark. I'm dressed in a tank top and shorts—the first time in months that I've had a stitch of clothing on after midnight.

That's okay. Even with Armand in bed two feet from me, I can't possibly think about sex right now. And not just because of the small, warm bundle nestled between us.

Poor Laura. She cried so much. And poor Armand, having to tell her. I saw how it ripped him up.

And now Armand is the Don. Which means that he's going to be a lot busier ... in a lot more danger ... and under a lot more scrutiny. Fuck.

My hand drifts to my belly, which is starting to feel taut and a little swollen. *This baby will come no matter what. And once I start showing, I don't know what's going to happen.*

I close my eyes. I can at least trust that Armand won't abandon me—he hasn't yet, has he? But first the baby ... and now this.

I'm running out of resilience, fast. But Laura needs me ... and the way he reaches across his daughter's body to bundle us both close to him makes it clear. Armand needs me too.

I'll just have to tough things out for now, and pray I don't fall apart.

I have never been to a funeral as lavish—or as crowded—as the one for Armand's father. There are literally hundreds of people crowding the reception hall afterward. I look after Laura, while Armand is all over the place handling things. His mother, her expression tired, chain smokes in the corner.

On our way out, I catch a glimpse of two men—the only ones at the hall not dressed in black—being wrestled into one of the black vans that drove out to the funeral and reception with us. I wait to ask about it until Laura is asleep later.

"The Frazettis are responsible for my father's death. Two came to lay a wreath that had a damn bomb in it. Don't worry—I handled it." He kisses the back of my neck and wraps his arms around me comfortingly.

"Holy shit," I mumble against the pillow, realizing that a big enough bomb would have taken out the first few rows of chairs. Where Laura and both of us were sitting.

"They never had a chance of getting close to us," he reassures again, and I gulp and nod, glad he can't see my face from behind.

Usually when he talks about his work, I can deal with it. But now people are dying, and people are planting bombs in the middle of crowds. And for the first time, I feel a tiny trickle of resentment. *How much weirdness—how much danger—am I expected to put up with here?*

He said I wouldn't have to deal with his ... work. But from the very first night, I have.

A few days later, a stressed-out Laura gets the sniffles. I care for her while she's sick because neither her father nor grandmother can risk getting sick right now. But within a few days, my throat starts to feel sore.

And the day after that, the worst cold of my entire life flattens me.

I've never had a cold hit me this hard. It has to be because of the pregnancy. And of course, since I'm pregnant, I can't take any cold medicine.

I spend two days sleeping it off and feeling useless

and lonely. Everyone has to keep their distance, leaving me mostly alone except when a servant comes in to serve me a meal or take the plate away. I spend my time drifting, body aching from the illness, or wrestling with troubled, fitful dreams.

At first, I keep my mood up. I know I'm pretty much quarantined until I've recovered. Armand can't afford to get sick, so of course he can't visit. I can barely talk anyway, my throat is so sore.

But eventually, it wears me down. I'm lonely, I'm tired, I'm everyone's last priority, and I just don't know what's going to happen to me beyond Armand's vague promises.

And that's when the resentment starts. It's just a little seed, deep inside my heart, sprouting in the hollow spot that craves Armand's love.

Where is Armand right now? The mother of his child is so sick, she can barely sleep from the muscle aches. But he doesn't so much as send me a text!

I'm being stupid and childish, and I damn well know it. I shouldn't be letting everything get the better of me like this. But as I lie there, my gaze again falls on the bed-stand drawer, and I think again, *how special am I to him, really?*

I don't know what to do besides cry myself to sleep. But eventually, when I wake up, I realize that if I have the energy to get myself worked up over a man, I have the energy to get up, take a shower, and take my damn temperature.

The aches and pains are gone, though I'm stiff from lying around in bed for two days. I take a long hot shower and drink two of the sports drinks I have stashed in my mini fridge. Then, finally, I get dressed and ready, and leave to go find Laura and my employers.

I'm wearing one of the new dresses that Armand has gotten me. It has an empire waist and flowing skirt, and should help hide my belly for a while. It's bright blue, a few shades lighter than my eyes.

I wonder if he'll even notice.

Where are you? Guards and staff bustle past, sometimes giving me nods. I smile awkwardly back and hurry on, headed for the stairs.

I am almost to the stairway landing when a small pink missile darts down the stairs and runs toward me, sobbing. Laura, pink dress rumpled and smudged, sees me and rushes over. She collides with me and wraps her arms around me, hiding her face against my belly.

It's not pleasant for my tender stomach, but I just gently hug her and stroke her hair. "What is it, sweetheart?"

"Grandma's yelling at Daddy and she won't stop! Then he started yelling too! I got scared and came down here." She turns her tear-streaked face up at me. "Did I do something wrong?"

"No, sweetie, there's no way. It's got to be something else." I hesitate. "Can you play in your room quietly while I go find out what's going on?"

"Will you come back soon?" she asks, calming down, only sniffling a little bit as she stares up at me.

"I will. And I'll tell you what I find out." Or I'll make up something sanitized enough for a little kid to hear.

I can't exactly hurry up to the top floor, where Armand's mother lives, but I make my way up as fast as I can. I'm sweaty and panting by the time I reach her floor, and have to stop to catch my breath. But I can already hear raised voices echoing down the hall.

Heart beating fast, I rush down there. Tony is standing outside the door, looking slightly pale. Few things rattle the big guy; it just upsets me more to see him that way.

He shakes his head when I come near the door, and says low, "Don't go in there, sweetheart. You'll get caught in the explosion."

I swallow back a nasty comment about how they've scared Laura and caught me up in this mess anyway. "What's going on?"

He lets out a sigh. "Listen for yourself. Is Laura okay?"

"Ran back to her room. I told her I would find out what the fight's about." Right now, I'm furious, and the look on my face seems to startle Tony.

He licks his lips and looks away awkwardly. "It's about you. I'm ... gonna go check on the kid, okay?" And off he walks down the hall, hands shoved in his pockets.

My anger dissolves and I draw a shivery breath. *Oh shit.*

I press my ear to the door and close my eyes, already knowing ... but still bracing myself.

"I can't believe that I'm over thirty and still having to listen to lectures about my sex life!" Armand shouts, more enraged than I have ever heard him. I flinch, but stand my ground, continuing to listen.

"I can't believe that you are over thirty and still have to have your mother keep an eye on your behavior! What are you planning to do with that poor girl now that you've gotten her pregnant? How are you going to explain this to Laura?" His mother's voice is raised too, but I can also hear the tears in it.

"It isn't any of your business! I've been taking care of the whole thing just like I promised her I would! I was handling it, Mother!" Armand's anger turns into exasperation.

"By talking that poor, innocent girl into bearing your bastard and hiding whose it is? What were you planning to do, pay her off? Daniela deserves better than that! And so does the baby in her belly!"

I freeze, suddenly having no idea whose side I'm on. On the one hand, I love Armand. On the other, his mother … is right.

Armand is silent for a long time. Then he says quietly, "She does deserve better. She deserves better than a guy who can't love her."

"Then you had better learn to love her, goddamn it, or so help me, everyone in the Five Boroughs is gonna know why!" And his mother bursts into tears.

I lean on the door, so dizzy and upset right now that I probably couldn't walk away if I wanted to. *What is she trying to force him into?* I remember her sticking her nose in at the beginning of our affair, her warning driving me to the decision to keep sleeping with her son.

I was like a rebellious teen then. And so was Armand …

"What the hell are you saying, Mother?" he asks in a shocked voice.

"I'm not having any bastards in this family because you can't control the brain in your pants around nannies. You are gonna marry that girl and treat her and your kids right. You are not gonna shame me or your father's memory by spending your adult life acting like a teenage boy!"

"You can't possibly be serious!" he complains at once. But then he goes quiet again, and a long, awkward silence stretches between them.

"It's the right thing to do," she insists. "And you damn well know it."

"What I know is that my decision about Daniela is just that—my decision!" he snaps back.

Tears fill my eyes. Suddenly, his selfishness is too much for me.

You prick. You seduce me, get me pregnant, keep me around with promises—and when your mom finally catches and calls you on it, you're so furious that you scare your daughter out of the room and bring your mom to tears. You're more concerned with keeping control than with what your actions do to the people who love you!

"You made your decision when you went against everyone's advice, started sleeping with another of our nannies, and then got her pregnant!" I hear a hard thud. "I even warned you this would happen, you stupid boy!"

"Wait, Mother, okay. Don't get out of bed, you'll fall again." Now Armand actually sounds worried and contrite, like he's figuring out just how much he's screwed up. "Look, I know you're upset, but why won't you let me handle this my own way?"

"Because you're not handling it, Armand," she sighs, and I gulp, tears brimming over. "You gotta marry that girl and make this right. If you're not going to think of her, think of the kid ... and your reputation with the Families."

Another long hesitation. And then, the resentment in his tone breaking my heart, he says a single word.

"Fine."

15

Daniela

Two weeks later, Armand and I are married in front of a priest. It's a quiet, private, somber affair, handled expediently—like a dirty chore he's getting out of the way. I don't invite any of my friends. I have no idea what I would tell them.

The whole time, Armand smiles only politely. He's kind to me, but even the kiss at the altar is as cold and perfunctory as the small crowd's applause. My heart sinks into my shoes and stays there, and as soon as I have a moment to slip off on my own at the reception, I lock myself in the bathroom and sob for a few minutes.

The sense that everything that I could possibly have had with Armand has now been ruined by this forced marriage haunts me as I smile and nod and talk stiffly through the rest of the reception. I don't even want to look his mother in the eyes, thanks to her part in this, and the way that Armand's all but openly sulking is starting to piss me off. But I weather my way through with the best fake smile I have.

The only people who look happy are innocent Laura, who gets to keep me now, and Armand's mother, who saunters around smugly, probably congratulating herself on putting things right. I can't confront her; I know the loss of her husband's still hanging over her. It might even be behind her sudden desperation to get the two of us hitched.

When Armand found me in my room to propose that day, he didn't know that I already knew he had been brow-beaten into marrying me by his mother. The first thing he did when offering me the simple gold band was to say, "I'm sorry."

He and I both know that he doesn't love me. He wants me to think he is marrying me to legitimize his child—and he is, but that wasn't his idea, either. I've been trying to console myself with the thought that a wealthy, virile husband with an adorable daughter is a fabulous catch, even if he doesn't love me.

It's more than my mother ever got, after all.

But I can already tell that things are going to get worse. The electricity between us is gone; he barely glances my way during the reception. When we drive home, he's tense and we barely speak.

He has no time for honeymoons. I have no heart for one.

When we get to my room, he doesn't touch me. He simply says, "You're the wife of the Don now. You're going to have certain duties besides looking after Laura and our children."

His voice is all business. It's the same tone he uses with his men downstairs.

I swallow my tears. "I understand."

He outlines his expectations. Meetings, social visits, church, improving my Italian. Our child must be christened. I sit there numbly, absorbing the information without really hearing my lover's voice behind them, and nod obediently.

Then he says in a more regretful tone, though still remaining cool, "The Frazettis tried to make another move during the wedding. We caught three more of their men. I have to go handle it."

But it's our wedding night! I blink up at him, so stunned and unhappy that I don't know what to say. Finally, I simply nod and close my eyes, lowering my head in resignation.

I manage to keep the tears back until he walks out and shuts the door. Then I look down at the cold bands of gold on my finger and yank them off, flinging them into the corner. I cry off my mascara into the sleeve of my wedding dress, aching from the loss of my lover.

He's not my lover anymore, after all. He's now my reluctant husband. And I am his ball and chain.

16

Armand

I hear Daniela—my new wife—start crying as soon as I close the door, and have to force myself to walk away. Shame and anger gnaw at my chest as I stomp back to my room to change out of my wedding tuxedo. After almost a month of nonstop tension and a sexual slowdown between Daniela and me, I was hoping to reconnect with her by at least being able to offer up some really choice wedding-night sex.

Instead, I pass along the lecture my mother gave her so that there will be no surprises. Then I apologize for my absence and leave. And I can see how much it hurts her. How much I hurt her, standing in the place of a proper husband, with no real love to offer.

I'm a burden to her now. She's married to this life, to the

Mob, to constantly having a target on her back. And she's stuck with someone who feels like he'll be betraying his dead wife if he loves anyone else.

Jesus, Mother's right. I really did screw up.

But this time, it's Carlo that's screwing things up.

The reason I can't even spend my wedding night with my new wife is that another crew of Carlo's tried to make sure that I didn't have one. Their orders were to take out Daniela to demoralize me. And I'm mad as hell about it as I change into my black suit and pull on a fresh pair of leather gloves.

I can't give her what she deserves. But I can keep her safe.

Tony catches up with me on the stairs again, like he's got a homing beacon. "Two more guys tried to run our van off the road transporting the guys here. I checked and they had trackers on them. Took the liberty of sending one of the boys to attach them to a jumbo jet at LaGuardia."

I snort, but even the idea of Carlo's guys going on a wild goose chase to another state, looking for where we're keeping his men, can't lift my mood. "You collected them all then?"

"One died in the crash. The other's ready for questioning downstairs with the first three. We already checked them for pills." He frowns as he trots down the stairs beside me. "You doing okay?"

Tony's the only one besides my mother who knows the whole score, so I speak a little on it. I can use my anger as fuel for what has to be done downstairs.

"Tony, I just had to marry a sweet, innocent girl who deserves eight thousand times better than me. She deserves someone who doesn't still reach for his dead wife across the bed every goddamn morning." I heave a huge sigh as we reach the second-floor landing. "Not to mention that instead of spending the next two hours fucking her, I'm stuck doing this shit."

"Hey, man, you know—I know the girl now. She really cares about you! You think she's not gonna understand that you'll need time to get over what happened to Bella? Come on!" His voice pleads, full of sympathy—and that's the only reason I don't let my irritation with him show.

"She shouldn't have to wait for me to be able to love her right. She's got nobody in the world but us—that's why she came here in the first place—and now that baby in her belly. Nobody." My voice is a growl, but under it all, the thought of disappointing Daniela feels like an icicle in my gut. "None of this should have happened."

"Seems to me you already care for her a whole damn lot," Tony says quietly, and I look back at him as we descend into the basement.

"It's not good enough. She deserves better. She deserves everything."

"Then maybe you need to let go of the idea that you're letting down B—"

The icicle stabs deeper into my gut and I turn a warning look on Tony. "There's no time for this now," I say simply, and he sighs and nods, falling into step just behind and beside me as we head down the basement corridor.

This time, we're using the big room at the far end. When I walk in, I'm looking at twenty prisoners—a quarter of Frazetti's men. We've put ten more in their graves. It's been a productive month.

I walk to the front of the room and look up at them, all shackled to their bolted-down chairs. At the sight of me, the new catches try to rattle me with glares and curses, while the veterans tense up and watch me wordlessly. I turn a look of icy rage on them all and the whole crowd goes quiet and still.

"Today, your psycho of a boss decided to try to interrupt my wedding with a van full of explosives and two snipers manning the back exit. We caught you. He loses again." I give them a humorless smile.

"Not for long, motherfucker," growls one of the new guys, a broad, muscular man in a bad suit whose hair is streaked with blond. I turn to him as the men around him wince and lean as far away from him as they can. Maybe they're worried about blood splatter.

"Oh really, not for long? Why? What exotic bullshit plan has Carlo cooked up this time? Did he pack your ass with C4 and put a trigger on your dick? Or do you plan to kill me with body odor?"

The guy shuts up suddenly, going dark red. Nervous laughter ripples through the captives, while my guys—facing them with assault rifles—snicker to each other. But I'm so pissed off right now that I'm suddenly on a roll.

"No, no, no. Let's explore this. This fucker seems to know all the answers, so let's hear them." I whip out my heavy revolver from under my suit coat and aim it right at the blond bastard's head. "Start talking."

His jaw drops and his eyes widen. "I—I—I only know my orders! Firebomb the place from the front, drive everyone out the back, and pick her and as many of your men off as we could with the snipers."

I thumb the hammer back. "I already know all of that. Not good enough."

"Holy fucking shit!" He's the color of pork fat now, gobs of sweat beading on his broad forehead, his eyes wide and his lips trembling. "Please. Mr. Rossini, he's got ... they, they've got—"

"Shut up or he'll fucking kill them!" a burly, olive-skinned guy with a buzz cut hisses at him. He goes very still when I swing my aim his way.

"You shut the hell up." I point at the blond. "Keep talking."

And the big punk collapses suddenly into something I didn't ever fucking expect. "He's got our families, sir! That's how he fucking recruits so fast!"

I lower the gun. "Wait. He's got your families?" I can't believe I'm hearing this correctly ... not because it doesn't make sense, but because it suddenly does in the most horrible way possible.

The scared young husband and father who was one of Frazetti's punks just moments ago nods, tears in his eyes. "I've got a wife and a one-year-old I haven't even gotten a phone call from in two weeks. I don't know where they are or what he's doing to 'em—I swear to God!"

I look around. Most of the men are very pale now, some with their mouths working in helpless anger. "All of you? He's keeping loved ones hostage for each and every one of his men?"

All of them nod. Every damn one.

"That's how the fucker keeps your loyalty?" I think about how close Laura came to being a hostage herself, and my fury shifts its target so decisively that I have to act.

"Look, man," the one who tried to silence his

coworker says in a steady voice. "Nobody here would go against you guys for him if he didn't have a gun to the heads of our loved ones. Respect, all right? But we can't tell you shit. My little man ain't even four."

I holster my pistol. "I am not gonna make you give up your boss if it endangers your families. I'm not going to do anything to endanger them at all."

Another ripple goes through the crowd. Most of them are looking at me in confusion. Some are suspicious.

"I'm going to free them. And once that's done, you guys are gonna help me kick him off this fucking planet."

My passionate statement shocks everyone, even me. Tony even leans over to me. "You sure about this, boss?" he asks quietly.

"This whole time we've been wondering how he gets so much loyalty out of his new recruits so damn fast. Now we know." I look around at the men, some of whom now have the faintest glints of hope in their eyes.

"I want every man in this room to know that I will make good on my promise to get your loved ones out of Carlo Frazetti's hands and to a safe place of your choosing, well away from here. And when I do that, you will have a choice. You can join them, or you can join me." I fold my arms across my chest.

They're all muttering to themselves and each other. I turn to Tony. "Have them all taken back to their cells to think about it. Tend any wounds and get them fed."

"We're filling up fast down here," Tony warns me.

"I know. It doesn't matter. Now that I know that Carlo doesn't have a single man who's loyal to him except by blackmail, I know that he's only bothered by the loss of manpower. He doesn't give a shit about his guys."

"So, what then?" Tony asks as we head back up to my rooms.

"Booze." I sigh. "And tomorrow, I put out the order to everyone to bring me Alexandra Frazetti, alive and unhurt."

"You're not gonna go spend the rest of your wedding night with your new wife?" he asks me very pointedly, both his eyebrows up.

"I left her crying, Tony," I sigh. "She probably hates me right now."

"She wouldn't be crying if she hated you." His dark eyes are much too piercing right now.

I close my eyes and pause a moment, feeling that icicle in my gut again. "I don't deserve her," I manage quietly. "Right now, I feel like I would just get her dirty."

He shakes his head. "Fine. Have it your way. But you're making a mistake."

17

Daniela

Armand hasn't touched me in weeks.

He's been sleeping down the hall in his lavish bed, while I still sleep right next to his daughter and look after her. Sometimes I get a kiss good night, and it seems like he wants to do more—but then he pulls away and leaves me alone. The pain isn't fading; I can't get used to it.

I knew it. I've been forced on him and now he resents it so much that he doesn't even want me in his bed anymore. He reassures me that I've done nothing wrong, and that I deserve the best. But then he gives me even less than before.

He's not cruel. He's supportive of my relationship with Laura, he gives me gifts, and he's encouraging me to keep painting.

But everything that comes from my brush looks like garbage. Muddy reds and sickly greens, roiling clouds of ugly color, landscapes full of dead things. My broken heart bleeds on the canvas, and the results are hideous.

I hide the canvases away at the back of the drying racks, high enough that Laura can't possibly reach them, and hope that nobody else notices them. I know why it's happening. I can fake a smile all day long, but painting comes from my heart and soul—and both are hurting.

Now and again, Armand needs me for something besides looking after Laura. Entertaining guests—mostly distant relatives from Sicily. My Italian is getting good enough that I can keep up a proper conversation. My acting skills are good enough that I look serene and poised, even with the ache of abandonment running through me.

I'm the new Don's wife on those days. Not Daniela. I know that supposedly makes me one of the most powerful women in New York ... but I don't feel powerful.

I feel like I'm just doing yet another job, on a much higher pay grade.

But on those lonely, empty nights, I still dream of Armand. His smile, his touch, his body against mine. The music of his groans, his tender whispers.

And I wake up flailing in the dark, reaching for him across the empty bed, so close to climax that I ache for it. And he's not there ... and my desire and relief turn into tears.

I'm into my second trimester when Armand's mother corners me unexpectedly while I'm wandering the garden for exercise. My feet and ankles are ridiculously swollen; I feel fat, weak, and depressed, and I'm hoping the walk will help. When I hear her voice behind me, I'm so exhausted emotionally that all I can do is roll my eyes quietly before turning around.

"Well, good afternoon, Daniela. How's my granddaughter doing?" She reaches for my growing baby bump without asking and I move back slightly, feet crunching on the dead leaves.

"She's been very active," I murmur, avoiding her eyes. *Don't fucking touch me, you overbearing old harpy.* "I'm having some problems with pain."

Not in my belly, though. The pregnancy thus far has been "flawless" according to the obstetrician. I work hard to keep it so, controlling everything I take in, getting exercise, staying hydrated.

Of course, that's all she's interested in. "Is the baby all right?"

"She's fine. I'm not." I don't want to tell her how her crusade for a legitimate grandchild has fucked up my life. So I'm vague, letting her assume it's my body and not my heart.

"Oh, that's too bad. Still nauseated?" She nods back with a pitying look as I nod. "First pregnancies are always the hardest. Don't you worry, you'll get the hang of it after the second one or so."

Ugh. "Thanks for the reassurance," I say in the most calm, cordial voice I can muster.

Meanwhile, deep inside, my heart aches again at the reminder of my cold, empty bed. Armand has become an expert at burying himself in his work. I only ever see him anymore when he needs me to be part of an event, or when he comes up to see Laura while I'm with her.

The first time Tony showed up and awkwardly told me that he was taking me to the doctor, I cried in front of him. Now, my game face is on all the time.

I stare back at my mother-in-law impenetrably. Her smile loses some of its strength, and then she forces it to widen again. "I only want to look after you both, my dear."

"Thank you," I reply, gentle, calm, and measured. I continue my walk, and she strolls beside me stiffly, leaning on a cane.

She speaks up brightly again after a few paces. "Anyway, I couldn't help but notice that you and my son do not sleep in the same room."

I stop dead. *Goddamn nosy cow. You didn't just.* But she did.

"My husband is working very hard to bring Mr. Frazetti to justice," I say in a softly resigned tone. "We end up going to bed at very different times."

"It's nice that you're covering for him, but every single night?" She peers down at me with those prying black eyes ... and suddenly, after months of holding it in, I snap.

"Yes, every single night. Not that it is any of your business." I throw up my hands. "You already got what you wanted! He's married and there's a baby on the way. Mission accomplished—now please, don't pry about our sex life!"

"But you can't possibly be happy this way!" She sounds genuinely confused ... as if she's so blind to the damage she's done that she actually thinks she's doing the right thing. Still. With my bed cold for months.

"Of course I'm not happy," I snap. "Of course! It's miserable knowing that the only reason he married me is because you forced him into it!"

Her jaw drops in astonishment. For a moment, as she stares at me, I think—fear, hope—that she might finally have understood.

But then she simply smiles tightly again. "You're just pregnant, and it's affecting your moods. It's all right, I don't take it personally."

And she turns around and strolls away as if nothing happened.

I stare after her … and hate her even more. I realize now that she won't ever admit that she was wrong to shove Armand and me together.

That night, Armand surprises me by stopping in to dine with us. Laura has started insisting on taking her meals with me, except when she's out with her father or grandmother. She says that I'm alone too much, and that makes her sad.

So now, if Armand wants to see his daughter at meals, he has to see me too, no matter how much of a burden I've become to him. I'm glad for Laura's adorable willfulness. I refuse to simply disappear into the woodwork of his home because Armand finds me inconvenient.

I eat quietly while he catches up with Laura, trying to ignore my sinking heart. "So, Halloween is coming up," he says to her brightly as he cuts her roast beef for her. "Do you know what holiday comes after that?"

"Turkey Day!" she replies cheerfully.

"And after that?" He's beaming at her. Now and again, he glances my way—and his smile fades a little, strengthening again only when he looks away.

"Christmas!"

I choke down another bite of roast. I haven't had enough protein today, and this is the last meal where

I'll have a chance to fix that. So I eat mechanically, trying to ignore how sick Armand ignoring me makes me feel.

"Yeah, sweetie. So you need to start thinking about a Christmas list for Santa. I know how long it takes you to decide on stuff like that." He winks at her, and she giggles.

I stare at the two of them as if from behind a layer of cold glass, with no idea how to find a way into the conversation. My growing belly is heavy on my thighs. I lay my free hand over the top of my bump, and sigh.

At least I'll have the baby soon; maybe then I won't be so damn alone.

Once he puts Laura to bed, Armand shocks me again by asking me to take a walk with him. Instead of going down to the moonlit garden, though, he takes me to the studio.

When I get there, the horrifying canvases that I tucked away lie along one wall in a makeshift display. "I can see why you put these up where Laura couldn't get at them," he says softly as walks up to stand in front of them.

You bastard. "Those were private," I start.

He eyes me. "I'm your husband."

I look down at the generic-looking gold bands on my finger. Every night before bed I take the rings off and shove them in the drawer with the condoms. Every morning before I leave the room, I put them back on. But they're the only real evidence that exists that I'm married.

"Not that anyone would notice," I say finally, tired of hiding all my inconvenient pain from him. "And those were still private. You should have asked."

He winces ... and then steels himself and gestures at the paintings. "What the hell is all this?"

I stare at him. "It's how I feel."

Armand looks from me to the paintings, his eyes widening in disbelief and more than a little anger. "This? This is how you feel? About what?"

I stare at him, struggling to put my crushing depression and loneliness into words. "Life."

"Life? You hate your life this much? You think your life's so miserable?" Now he's really angry, and defensive. And he goes off.

"You live in a fucking palace. You share my money and even some of my power. Nobody's ever gonna question the legitimacy of your kid, and neither you nor she will ever want for anything. What more do you want?"

It takes all my willpower not to scream at him. Instead, I fold my arms across my chest and stare at him. "You've avoided me since we got married and now your mother has noticed we don't ever sleep in the same bed. Guess who she decided to nag about it?"

The anger leaves his face and he blinks at me. "What?"

I tell him about the encounter in the garden. He scowls and shakes his head when I'm done.

"My mother has a problem with boundaries. I will talk with her." He hesitates, then asks, "What really has you upset enough that you're painting like … this?"

"You've abandoned me," I say softly. My voice is so faint that for a moment I don't think he heard me.

He turns to me. "I thought you wanted me to."

I let out a thin, sad laugh. "No. I don't know why you always make excuses not to visit me anymore, but it's not because of anything I said or did."

His gaze lowers slightly, a puzzled look crossing his face. "We were forced together by circumstances. You seem so unhappy about it."

"I'm really fucking lonely, Armand," I say softly. "What you offered me wasn't perfect, but what you're doing now is even less."

He looks at me in disbelief, his defenses going up again. "You can't tell me that you would have willingly settled for marrying and having kids with a guy who is still mourning his dead wife."

"Yeah, actually, I would have. Because she's someone you loved, not my competition!" I don't know if Bella and I would have gotten along, but I don't see her that way.

I plow on, not knowing what else to do. "I ... I was willing, you know. To put up with the whole 'great sex and friendship' thing and not let my feelings for you grow too much. And then I was willing to deal with my pregnancy quietly, while you figured out what to do. And then, when you came to tell me you couldn't have a bastard child, I agreed to marry you. Even though I knew you didn't love me, or want me as a wife."

He stares at me, and after a little struggling, I go on. "I have done everything that you wanted, the way you wanted. And now, in return, you've abandoned me. You don't touch me, you barely talk to me—you barely look at me most of the time."

He blinks slowly. "I got you pregnant and trapped in this life. I really did think that you hated me."

"You never asked how I felt," I whisper, so full of anger and pain inside that I'm scared it will boil over and I'll start screaming at him after all. "You just assumed."

He looks down, and says the same thing he did when he proposed. "I'm sorry."

"Yeah," I whisper, wishing that he would at least reach across the gap between us and put an arm around me. *Just touch me.*

Instead, he moves away slightly. "You've given me a lot to think about. I won't look at your work again without asking."

I nod, choking on the lump in my throat.

My heart feels like it's going to crack as he turns to leave ... but then he hesitates, standing framed in the doorway. "I'm ... glad you don't hate me. And I ... I can't fucking say anything else for sure right now because everything has gotten so goddamn crazy."

He gives me a soft look, one full of pain. "I haven't come near you because I don't want to mess things up worse. There isn't anyone else, and believe me, I've been aching for you. But I feel like shit when I think about coming down here to sleep with you."

"I don't get it. We're married. Why would you feel guiltier now than you did before?" I stare at him, and he sighs through his nose.

"Because now you're stuck with me." He seems to think that's a bad thing. The guilt in his eyes confuses me.

"What if I like that idea?" I urge quietly. "What if I'm okay with giving you some time to mourn Bella? Could you at least stop ... acting like I don't exist?"

He nods awkwardly. "Well, I can do that. But with the Frazetti mess, things aren't going to be very normal for a while."

I feel a strange little thread of hope now. He's not acting like he hates me. He's just asking for time and room to sort himself out. "I'm ... glad to hear you don't hate me."

He smiles sadly. "Never could."

"But what about your mom? That situation today really messed with me." *Are we talking things out?*

He gives me an apologetic wince. "My mother's been half out of her head since Dad died, but that's no excuse for how she's been acting. I'll tell her to leave you alone."

"Thank you."

He almost turns away again, but then almost blurts out, "You gotta know ... it's not you. If you and I had been left alone, we could have sorted things out. If I had met you in a few years, after some more distance from Bella's death ..."

I smile at him through my tears. "I get it. Just ... don't leave me alone so much, okay?"

He nods back, a little more light in his eyes. "Okay."

18

Armand

It's a rough winter. Alexandra's gone to ground. I've got specialists tracking her, but nothing yet.

Cooped up in the house, we can't get away from my mother's nosiness and endless meddling. I have to shoo her away from Daniela multiple times; her hunger for another grandchild has her ignoring my wife's comfort and boundaries entirely. And every time I shoo her off, we end up in an argument.

But it's worth it, because at least Daniela's less unhappy.

There's a crib and playpen in Daniela's room now, and a closet full of maternity clothes. She's getting huge. The kid's healthy. They're giving us a due date of early to mid-March.

We're getting along better, too. It's not like it was before the wedding, but she's no longer acting like she can't stand to be in the same room with me.

Lovemaking is off the table for now, for reasons besides all the shit going on between us. Daniela's belly is big and sensitive. My dick feels like it's going to explode sometimes from disuse, but I can curl around her from behind at night, and bury my face in the back of her neck, and we both sleep well again, together.

Laura's grown another half inch in six months. She's going to be tall and stately like her grandma—who might resent me, but is still getting more and more excited as Daniela's due date nears.

But the winter and the waiting are driving me crazy inside.

Finally, near the end of February, we get a break. One of my mercenaries who was sent after Alexandra brings me a very nice present.

"Where the hell did Carmela find her?" I ask as Tony and I hurry down to the basement. I'm still buttoning my shirt—he caught me just out of the shower.

"Mallorca. Under heavy guard. She came pretty quietly, too, once the guards were taken out. Says she wants to make a deal."

I walk into the interrogation room and see

Alexandra sitting there wearing a tired, worried expression—totally different from her usual icy haughtiness. She's in a surprisingly plain white dress, hair up in a simple ponytail, and when she sees me she almost tries to get up from the chair. "I gotta talk to you!" she cries.

"Yeah, I heard." I don't touch my weapon, and don't stand over her. I stop a bit away instead. "What the hell's going on?"

"You gotta help me get away from my father!" she says—and those usually hard eyes brim over with desperate tears.

Tony and I exchange astonished looks, and then I nod at her. "Go on."

She talks. I listen. Sometimes I ask questions. Ten minutes in, the manacles are off and she's showing me the healing bruises on her arms and calves.

"He's been doing this since your mom died?" I ask in a steady voice. Nothing surprises me anymore with this guy.

"Yeah." She wipes her cheek. "I thought if I could make you like me, you'd help me."

I stare at her, her clumsy dick-check during the meeting making sense suddenly. "Oh shit. Honey, look, all you woulda had to do was slip me a damn note, okay?"

"No, I didn't know that!" she cries out shakily. "I'm

not used to guys like you and Tony, I'm used to guys like him! Like my father!"

"Oh God. Okay. I'm sorry." I hold my hands out, placatingly. "Look. I'll help you. I don't even have to keep you hostage as long as you're playing along that I am. Get what I'm saying?"

"Yeah," she breathes. "Kind of."

"I'll put you in a safehouse, you can stay out of circulation until I deal with your—with Carlo." I can't call him her dad. He's her abuser. "I'll need you to do some acting and make a scared phone call or two. And … I need some information."

Alexandra's always been a bitch. I didn't know it was armor. Right now, though, there's real determination on her smudged face. "Whatever I've got."

"I need to know where your father keeps the families of his men."

She nods at once. "In a warehouse in the Bronx. I've been there."

Once we send Alexandra off to a safehouse under heavy guard, Tony and I talk strategy.

"Jesus," Tony breathes, echoing my thoughts as we head up to the meeting room. I've called in every man available. "Carlo really doesn't have a single person in his life who's loyal—except out of fear. That's just … crazy."

"I know," I sigh. "But it's about to be his Achilles

heel. Those men we caught ... it's time to get them their families back."

Half an hour later, a cloak of silence isolates Carlo's warehouse. We cut their hard lines and set up radio and phone jammers. We black out the neighborhood for a while to cover our way in. And we let our new recruits lead the way.

The guards see a bunch of Frazetti's men coming and don't even unholster their weapons. Blondie's the first to grab one and take him hostage. "Don't you fucking move, Joey!"

"Mike, what the hell? What is this?"

"I want my wife and my baby back, that's what. And that goes for all of us." He jabs the smaller man in the temple with his pistol. "Now open the fucking cages!"

"I can't," he mumbles, eyes widening as I come strolling up. "They've got my wife too."

"Look, the thing you're not getting here is that 'they' is *you*," I say very patiently. "This is your chance to take your family and get the fuck away from this mess with your skin intact. Now, do you take it, or do you die for a piece of shit like Carlo?"

He turns around, punches in the code, and lets us in.

Inside, it's chaos. But to my amazement, it's happy chaos. The warehouse is lined with cages with women, kids, and older people in them. The men—some of them still in uniform, having turned instantly when given the chance—are unlocking the cages, some of them getting impatient at the lack of key copies and using bolt cutters on the locks instead.

"This was a hell of a risk," Tony says.

I nod. "Worth it, though. Any resistance?"

He shakes his head. "Took the building without a shot fired. I tell you, man, your dad would be proud."

I smile back. "Yeah, I hope so."

He puffs out his cheeks, looking around. "You know, you just removed all his leverage against his men, and as far as he knows, you have a gun to his daughter's head. You know he's gonna retaliate."

"He's gonna try. But at this point, he'll have to pick up a gun and do it himself." I flash a grin. "And it's gonna be a little bit before he knows that. Once his bodyguards get the calls from their wives that we're gonna help them make, they'll either quit or shoot the fucker themselves."

"That's gonna take a while. He doesn't let his guys wear personal cells on duty." Mike's stuck around. He has a smiling, bruised lady cradled in one arm and a disheveled but grinning toddler in the other.

I stifle a curse the moment I see the kid, and Tony snorts and rolls his eyes. I poke him with my elbow. "Okay, that gives us some lag time. But by tomorrow morning, this should all be over with."

I'm wrapping the mission up and getting ready to go home when my phone rings. It's my mother. "Everything's all right at home?" I ask at once.

"Daniela's water broke," comes the matter-of-fact reply. "And you need to come home now."

"Holy shit." I signal to Tony, who turns and jogs out to the car to bring it around for me. "How is she doing? Put her on the phone!"

"Oh, she's already at the hospital," she says blithely. "But you need to come home now."

I freeze, blood running hot and cold in turns. "What are you saying?"

"Carlo gave me a call. He's gotten hold of Daniela's medical info, including her admission status just now. He's sending men to kill you all. Don't go." Her voice is faint and strangely hollow.

"You think I'm gonna leave my wife and child defenseless to save my own skin?" My heart starts beating very hard, and for a single, terrifying moment, I'm glad my mother isn't in front of me. I might actually strangle her.

"You are the Don. We need you. Laura needs you. You can have another baby. And another nanny." She sounds so terribly reasonable ... so calm. So insane.

"I'm going," I snap—and she explodes.

"No! No, you come home! You come home now, you ungrateful little boy! You are not risking your life and this family's hold on the city for some servant you knocked up!"

"I'm hanging up on you now, Mother, before you say anything else we'll both regret." And I do, in the middle of her screaming at me. And even though my mind's racing with the thought of Daniela in danger, I have to admit that it feels pretty good.

But I can't linger on that. I turn to Mike. "I need your help."

He nods once. "Anything."

19

Daniela

All the breathing exercises and core strengtheners in the world haven't prepared me for this. I'm delirious even after the epidural, my head pounding, the remnants of pain still haunting me from neck to knees. The nurses mill around me, checking instruments, checking my dilation, and every time one comes by, I have to fight the urge to beg her to knock me out entirely.

I don't know where Armand is. His mother promised to call him and let him know. That was half an hour ago. Terror is starting to gnaw at me, thinking that I might have to do this alone.

Does he not care? Could he not get away? Or was she being two-faced, and didn't tell him at all?

Another contraction ripples through me, and I pull

in huge huffs of air. *Armand had barely left with his men when I started feeling it. Maybe he's still out on the job and just doesn't know yet.*

But how long will he be gone? I'm so scared. I don't want to go through this alone.

But my body doesn't give a damn about any of that, and soon I can barely think of anything outside of wrestling with my fear and pain.

One of the doctors is at my elbow. His voice sounds soothing but barely eases me. "You're dilating pretty fast. Fetal heart rate's fine. We're going to be monitoring both your vitals from the other room until your contractions get closer together."

"Okay," I manage.

He finishes up and walks out. And I drift. A while later, I hear footsteps come in the door.

"Armand?" I raise my head hopefully—and stare in shock at the man in the doctor's coat who is pointing a gun at me.

"Sorry," he says.

My blood goes to ice as he closes the door behind him and approaches me, pistol first. "What ... why ..."

"It's nothing personal," he mumbles. He can't look at me. "If it was my choice, lady, for what it's worth ... I wouldn't even be here."

"That's some pretty cold fucking comfort when you're pointing a gun at me," I choke out, trying to buy time. All I need is for someone to walk in and raise the alarm. *Please.*

"I know. Look, it's ... Frazetti. Nobody likes him—we don't do this shit because we like it either." It's like he's apologizing for even being here. "He's got my ma."

I stare at him. "Hostage?"

He feels so guilty about killing a pregnant woman in labor that I can see his gun wavering even as he stammers out his explanation. "Yeah. That's why I gotta shoot you. I'm really sorry, lady."

I can scream for help ... but if this guy's being forced anyway, neither he nor his boss will much care if he gets out of here alive. I stare at him, shivering, and another contraction rips through me, making me cry out in pain.

The door slams inward.

For a moment I can't make out the black outline that strides through the too-bright doorway. But then I hear his voice—Armand's voice—brimming over with white-hot fury. "You get the hell away from my wife!"

The man with the gun turns—and points it at Armand, who just walks in with his pistol in one hand and a cell phone in the other. "Don't come any fucking closer!"

"Take it easy," Armand says in such a cold, controlled voice that some of my terror ebbs away. "You got a choice here, Danny Cortese."

The guy stiffens. "How do you know my name?"

"One of your coworkers told me which of Carlo's goons we hadn't reached yet. We narrowed it down while we were processing all of his hostages."

I can tell from the set of Danny's shoulders that he's shocked. "Wait, you did what?"

"There's a nice lady on the other end of this phone line that I set free half an hour ago, and she'd like to talk to her son. But he only gets the phone if he puts his fucking gun away. Otherwise, he's gonna get a bullet."

Danny starts to gasp for air. "That can't be right. There's no way you could free all of them; even we couldn't figure out how to do that—"

Armand shrugs and hits the speakerphone button.

"Danny?" comes a nervous, quavering voice. "Danny, are you okay? Please don't do anything foolish, Danny. I'm fine. These nice men came and rescued us."

He drops the gun onto a chair and lunges forward, snatching up the phone. "Ma? Ma? Are you okay?" He hurries out the door, so distracted that he walks right past Armand.

Armand, who could have shot him easily, just chuckles and holsters his gun under his suit coat. Then he hurries over to my side and bends over me. "Hey, sweetheart. Sorry I'm late."

"You were out ... rescuing a bunch of people?" It

sounds like something he would do—but it doesn't sound like something a mobster would do, leaving me pleasantly surprised.

"Well ... yeah." He smiles warmly and a bit awkwardly. "How are you doing?"

"I'm in labor. And some guy just pointed a gun at me. Can we go on a vacation soon? I'm tired of all of this!" Another contraction hits, and I whimper.

He gives me his hand to squeeze and smooths my sweaty hair back. "Just name where, and I'll make it happen. Let's just get through this first."

"What happened with ... I mean ..."

"Carlo's finished. Even his own daughter despises him. If someone close to him doesn't end him soon, one of the enemies he's made will." He bends down and kisses my forehead, and then my lips, tenderly.

"You came just in time," I murmur, so grateful that fresh tears spring to my eyes.

"I should have been here from the beginning." He settles into the chair next to the head of my hospital bed. "But I'm here now. And I'm not going anywhere, baby."

20

Daniela

"Okay, so whose turn is it for presents?"

Christmas has come around again—my first Christmas ever as both a mother and a wife. We had our lavish extended-family Christmas already, and I even managed to ignore his mother's overly personal questions and keep the peace.

But this? This is ours.

Armand's cabin in the Catskills is on twenty acres of meandering land through the mountains. Armand's dad kept it as a hunting lodge. Now, it's our cozy winter retreat.

Laura is now six and growing like a weed. I adopted her officially a few months ago, silently promising Bella to do the best I can. She's a lot happier and more energetic than when I was first hired on as her nanny, and she loves her new baby sister.

Right now, she's painting away at her new easel on her new art pad, using her new brushes. She'll need them. We're back to painting in the studio together regularly, and my landscapes are happy again.

Audrey, wiggling excitedly in my arms, will be turning one in three months. She's a sweet-faced little cherub who adores her big sister, and her blue-gray baby eyes are already showing hints of gold and green.

Armand has a Santa hat on his head that Laura plunked there, wearing it gamely with his suit. "Looks like Audrey got something!" And he wiggles a purple plush bear at her.

Audrey squeals and kicks and grabs for the bear clumsily, then immediately shoves its paw in her mouth and starts chewing.

"Why's she eating the bear?" Laura blinks up at her kid sister from her easel.

"It's a baby thing. That's why she doesn't get to go near your paints." I tug the paw loose from Audrey's mouth and pop a binky in instead.

But Armand isn't done yet. He comes over and hands me a small box. "This one's overdue," he says cryptically, and sits back on the couch to watch me open it.

I hesitate for a moment, then unwrap it. It's a ring

box. Inside, a white gold wedding set with a wisteria pattern gleams back at me.

I stare between it and him. *Oh my God.*

It's been a lot of time and work to get us here—vacationing safely, with neither Armand's job nor his mother causing problems. And we're together—really together, after all this time. "It's beautiful."

Carlo is gone. He was found floating facedown in the East River by sanitation workers. Nobody knows who did it—it could even have been his daughter.

Armand told me that half the Frazetti men skipped town with their families, and the rest now work for us. Carlo's daughter inherited a pile of money and disappeared. And we all breathed a big sigh of relief.

While that was one obstacle out of our way, Armand's mother still tries to be a problem sometimes. She wants to try to tell me how to parent the girls. Sometimes, she starts quizzing me again on things she shouldn't. Then Armand steps in and threatens to put her in a home if she doesn't stop hassling me, and she sulks off.

She'll sulk even more when she sees these rings.

"I never got to pick you out anything special, you know, back when we got married. I wanted to fix that. So you like it?"

I smile and lean over to kiss him. "It's beautiful."

"Not as beautiful as you," he replies, cupping my cheek. "I love you, you know."

I smile into his eyes and nod, thinking back to how impossible those words seemed just a year earlier. It may have taken some time, and it may have been a bumpy road, but ever since Armand came to realize that he loves me, he doesn't go a day without telling me so.

Later, once the girls are in bed, we curl up on the couch for a while. "You think you can handle the big New Year's party?" he asks gently as he nuzzles my hair. "Wouldn't blame you if you said no—I know you're tired from chasing the kids."

"I can do it." I lean my head against his broad shoulder, and he kisses my temple.

"Good. I'll make sure to sneak you off once it tolls midnight." He winks and then leans over to kiss me lingeringly.

As we undress by the firelight and caress each other, I can't help but think of that first day that I met Armand. Back then, I was just a desperate, ordinary girl looking for an honest job—and he was a horny flirt of a widower.

People change. They grow. And they recover.

The Christmas lights hanging from the walls blur in my vision as he kisses my full, aching breasts and tongues my nipples erect. When he enters me, I hold him blissfully, and we rock together slowly in the multicolored glow.

Our love was a hard fight to start. But in the end, it was worth every tear.

The End.

ABOUT THE AUTHOR

Mrs. Love writes about smart, sexy women and the hot alpha billionaires who love them. She has found her own happily ever after with her dream husband and adorable 6 and 2 year old kids.

Currently, Michelle is hard at work on the next book in the series, and trying to stay off the Internet.

"Thank you for supporting an indie author. Anything you can do, whether it be writing a review, or even simply telling a fellow reader that you enjoyed this.
Thanks

©Copyright 2020 by Michelle Love - All rights Reserved

In no way is it legal to reproduce, duplicate, or transmit any part of this document in either electronic means or in printed format. Recording of this publication is strictly prohibited and any storage of this document is not allowed unless with written permission from the publisher. All rights are reserved.

Respective authors own all copyrights not held by the publisher.

 Created with Vellum

www.ingramcontent.com/pod-product-compliance
Lightning Source LLC
LaVergne TN
LVHW031604060526
838200LV00055B/4482